SARAH PURDUE

◆

LOVE'S LANGUAGE

Complete and Unabridged

LINFORD
Leicester

First published in Great Britain in 2016

First Linford Edition
published 2017

A catalogue record for this book is available
from the British Library.

ISBN 978–1–4448–3330–0

Published by
F. A. Thorpe (Publishing)
Anstey, Leicestershire

Set by Words & Graphics Ltd.
Anstey, Leicestershire
Printed and bound in Great Britain by
T. J. International Ltd., Padstow, Cornwall

This book is printed on acid-free paper

LOVE'S LANGUAGE

Sophie Carson has always dreamed of being a teacher, and now finally she has the chance. Due to start her training in Wales, there is only one problem: she must be able to read and write in Welsh. While studying, she works at the caravan site in Anglesey previously owned by her grandparents — and meets David, the heartbroken son of the new owners. Can Sophie convince him to help her with her studies, as she tries to help him mend his broken heart?

1

Maple's caterwauling had reached fever pitch and Sophie didn't think she could take much more. Thanks to a jack-knifed lorry on the M60 near Manchester, the journey from Kent had taken a whole three hours longer than the route planner had said it would. Sophie was tired and desperately in need of a toilet stop, and judging from the reproachful looks from Maple, Sophie was sure her cat felt the same. Maple, four years old, silky black fur and a princess attitude, sat beside her in the passenger seat. For the past hour Maple had rested her front paws up on the dashboard and sung so loudly that Sophie had given up and switched off the radio.

'We're nearly there, Maple, I promise. Maybe ten more minutes and then

1

you can get out and explore your new home.'

Sophie kept her eyes firmly fixed on the road in front but she could feel the feline's glare.

'And we'll get you that tin of tuna I've been promising you,' Sophie added, thinking, like all cat owners, that Maple could understand her every word. Out of the corner of her eye she watched Maple circle the seat a few times before finally sitting down and tucking in her tail and paws primly.

The narrow country lanes, bordered on both sides by fields of sheep and cattle, were so familiar to her, yet she felt like she had been away from them for years, which of course she had. She had planned on stopping at the local shop to pick up a few supplies on the way but what she and Maple needed right now was to get to their new home and start settling in. Unlike all the tourists who visited the Saint Peulan Campsite, Sophie knew exactly where the turn-off was, so was able to slow down and make the turn on the first attempt. She drove slowly past the sign, which looked new, and parked outside the small wooden hut that served as reception. Maple opened one eye and flicked her tail as Sophie got out of the car.

The small bell over the door jangled as she opened it and she was immediately taken back to all the summers she had spent at the campsite as a child.

'Welcome to Saint Peulan Campsite,' came the greeting from a man who looked to be about sixty. He was perched on a stool and resting one leg, encased in a plaster cast, on an upturned milk crate. 'Do you have a booking?'

He smiled warmly at her and Sophie felt some of the tension leave her. It had seemed like such a sensible plan to her, but her sister and all of her friends had not hidden the fact that they thought she was losing the plot.

'Actually, I'm Sophie. Sophie Carson?'

She held out a hand, realised that he couldn't reach it from where he was sat, and took a step forward.

'Sophie! Of course,' he said, shaking her hand. 'Welcome to your new home, or should I say welcome back?'

'Probably a bit of both,' she said with a smile.

'Jeff? Is that someone booking in?' a woman's voice called from the back room.

'It's Sophie, Gwen. She's arrived at last.'

A woman bustled out of the back room, dressed in jeans and a T-shirt with the campsite logo on it.

'Sophie! We were getting worried about you but I told Jeff it was probably traffic, so we tuned in the radio and heard about that lorry on the motorway. Poor you,' Gwen said with a warm smile that reminded Sophie of her mum. She fought down an unexpected wave of homesickness.

'I think Sophie probably just wants to get settled and make herself a cup of tea, love,' Jeff said gently in a way that suggested Gwen would go on talking given half the chance.

'Of course you do, Anywylyd. I'll get the keys. You know where to go?'

Sophie smiled at the familiar Welsh word.

'I do, thanks,' she said as Gwen handed her a set of keys on a keyring of the Welsh red dragon.

'Do you need any milk or tea?' Gwen said. 'Or I can put the kettle on if you want a cuppa first?'

'Thank you, but I've got my cat in the car. I'd really like to get her settled, but maybe I can pop back later and we can talk about work?'

Jeff waved his hand in dismissal.

'You've only just got here, pet, work can wait till tomorrow. You get yourself settled. If you need anything, just let us know.'

Sophie drove around the back of the hut to where the owners and workers of the campsite had their various caravans and mobile homes. She drove along the row, taking in how much camping life had changed since she was a child. Gone were the sun-bleached awnings and ancient beige caravans. Now there were silver bullet-shaped vans, with sides that popped out to give more room, satellite dishes and awnings with inflatable frames that looked like they could withstand the strongest Anglesey wind. At the end of the row were the two static caravans that were reserved for workers who didn't come with their own accommodation. Looking at them, Sophie was pretty sure they were at the end of their twenty-five-year life, but they still made her smile. She had spent many a summer living in them and it truly felt like she was coming home.

She glanced down at the keys and drove into the grass area that was her parking spot.

'We're here, Maple. This is home.'

As nonchalant as ever, Maple stretched lazily and got onto all four paws so she could see out the window

. . . just as the passenger door flew open.

'For goodness sake! You can't park here!'

Sophie didn't have time to shout a warning — Maple was up and out of the seat, speeding across the grass before disappearing into the wooded area that surrounded the campsite. Ignoring the irate voice, Sophie pushed open her door and ran in the direction that Maple had disappeared.

'Maple,' she called softly, knowing that shouting would only spook her pet more. 'Maple, come here sweetie.'

She crept forward, holding out her hand as she called, whilst desperately looking for any sign of her beloved pet.

'Didn't you hear me? I said you can't park here.' The voice was exasperated now and Sophie could tell without turning round that it was a man's voice. If you could tell by tone alone, Sophie would have put him at about her age, twenty-six. Momentarily, she was torn between telling this man exactly what he had done and ignoring him and continuing her search for Maple.

'Ignoring me won't help. If you don't move your car, I'll be forced to call the police.'

That was it. Sophie straightened up to her full height of five foot four and spun round.

'I think you'll find I can park here,' she said, gesturing at her car and the static caravan, 'because I live here. In fact, I work here, so if anyone is calling the police it will be me!' She didn't mean that last part, but had got a bit caught up in her own indignant attitude.

'Ah,' said the man, who, now Sophie looked at him, was definitely on the handsome side. He had caramel-brown hair that flopped into his eyes, which were a shade darker. 'Sorry, I didn't know we had someone new starting.'

Sophie arched an eyebrow.

'Perhaps you should check your facts before threating police action.'

'I work here too, so I guess the same

could be said for you, since you threatened to call the police on me.'

Now the handsome man arched an eyebrow but also crossed his arms. Sophie had to fight the urge to cross hers too.

'Well at least I didn't terrify your pet!' Sophie said. The thought of Maple being lost was bringing tears to her eyes and she tried to take a deep breath to fight them back.

'Pet?' he asked as if he was talking to someone who was mad.

'Yes, my cat. She was sat in the front seat and you scared her when you yanked open the door. Now she's somewhere out there, lost and . . . '

Sophie stopped talking, as she knew that if she carried on her voice would break, and the last thing she wanted to do was start bawling in front of a stranger. Particularly this stranger.

'Ah,' he said, and at least had the decency to look slightly sheepish. 'I can help you look, if you like?'

Sophie swallowed.

'No, thank you. I doubt she'll come out if you're around since you've already scared her today. The best thing you can do is leave.'

She dipped her head, a little embarrassed at her manner. She knew she was being unfair, it wasn't really his fault. She should have kept Maple in the cat carrier for the entire journey, but the creature had started making such a fuss during the traffic jam that she had let her out.

'Okay, but if you change your mind, just let me know.' He turned and walked away. 'I live next door,' he said over his shoulder, whilst pointing in the direction of the other static caravan.

Sophie groaned inwardly. Not the most auspicious start to making friends with the neighbours, but neither was it her most pressing problem right now. Right now, she needed to find Maple.

2

Sophie had been forcing herself to unpack and get settled. She had tried calling Maple, even left an open tin of tuna outside the back window of the caravan, in the hope that Maple would be coaxed out of hiding. She knew that the more she fussed the less likely it was that Maple would appear. That was the way with cats. It wasn't like owning a dog, who would come when you called; cats pretty much did what they wanted, when they wanted to, so all Sophie could do was wait.

She had emptied the boot of her car and found a place for everything. She hadn't brought a huge amount with her — the truth was, she didn't own a huge amount. There had never been a lot of money for more than the basics, and she had always been happy with her lot.

Cradling her cup of tea, Sophie sat

herself down on the ring of sofas that filled the entire back end of the caravan. She twitched the curtains to give herself a good view of the wooded area, hoping that she would spot the swish of a tail or a whisker. Maple had moved around a lot in her four years, so was used to finding her way home to her new residence. Even so, Sophie couldn't help but worry.

A hammering on the door made her jump. The walls of the caravan were so thin, it felt like the whole building was shaking. She jumped up, wondering if Gwen had come to pay her a visit to talk about work. She made a vain attempt to smooth down her hair and brush off some of the dust that had accumulated on her clothes and pushed open the door.

It was not who she was expecting. The handsome stranger, her neighbour and seemingly her fellow work colleague, was standing on the doorstep. He was tapping his foot in impatience and Sophie got the message loud and clear. Somehow, and she didn't know how, she had managed to annoy him, again. She tried a smile but it was not returned.

'I think I have something of yours,' he said. With a sigh, he held out his arm and indicated that Sophie should follow him. Not knowing what else to do, she made her way down the steps. When they were stood outside his caravan, the man stopped and indicated that Sophie should look through the small window by the kitchen area. Sophie could feel her heart in her mouth as she peeked through the window. Maple was curled up in a tight ball on the end of the bed that Sophie could see through the open bedroom door.

'Maple!' Sophie said. 'How did she get in there?'

'I have no idea, but she seems to have made herself at home.'

Sophie winced as there was no sign of any amusement in his voice.

'Thank you for coming to get me,' Sophie said, turning around. 'Look, I know we haven't got off to the best start, so maybe we could begin again?'

She held out her hand.

'I'm Sophie Carson. It's nice to meet you.'

The man stared at her outstretched arm, and for a heartbeat Sophie wondered if he was going to ignore her gesture. Finally, with no hidden reluctance, he reached out and shook her hand.

'David. David Monroe.'

Now it was Sophie's turn to raise an eyebrow. 'Monroe, as in Jeff and Gwen?'

'Yep, my parents,' he said with a shrug. Sophie could feel her brain trying to digest this new information.

'My grandparents used to own this place, so I spent a lot of time here as a child.'

'Poor you,' David said, and he seemed to mean it. Sophie frowned.

'Not at all. I loved it here. It's one of the reasons I've come back.'

David could not have looked more

surprised than if Sophie had struck him across the face, *à la* Scarlett O'Hara. They stood there, like they were posing for an old fashioned photograph. Sophie felt like she should fill the silence but she didn't know what to say. In the short time she had known David, she felt pretty sure that they had absolutely nothing in common.

'Right. Okay. Well . . . ' she said, turning her attention back to more important matters. 'Maybe I should take Maple now?'

David had been studying this strange woman who had moved in next door and was suddenly a little embarrassed, conscious that he may have been staring.

'Of course. She seems pretty settled, I think you should be able to pick her up easily enough.'

He gently pushed open the door and indicated that Sophie should go first. Sophie stepped into the caravan and was a little taken aback by the state of the place. To say it was untidy would be unfair to untidy people. Every surface had something on it, and that included dirty dishes and the remnants of takeaways. The floor was completely covered with clothes that needed washing, and more shoes than Sophie owned.

'Perhaps you could move a bit? Then I can come in too.'

Now it was Sophie's turn to feel embarrassed at the staring.

'Sorry,' she mumbled, and stepped into the bedroom.

Maple rolled on her back, all four paws in the air, and yawned. She looked the very picture of relaxed and at home.

'Maple, what are you doing here?' Sophie said softly, feeling both relieved that she had found her and somewhat embarrassed with her errant feline.

'Apparently, sleeping on my Jacque Terrard limited-edition cashmere sweater.'

Sophie had no idea who Jacque Terrard was, but she assumed from David's tone that he made ludicrously expensive clothing.

'I'm so sorry,' she said, reaching for Maple and pulling her into her arms. Maple for her part started purring and rubbing her head under Sophie's chin. 'I'll get it washed for you.'

'It's dry clean only,' David said icily, lifting the sweater and holding it up to the light through the bedroom window. Even Sophie could see the mat of black hairs coating the soft pink wool.

'I'll get it dry cleaned then,' Sophie said, wishing that she could magically transport herself to anywhere other than where she was right now.

'I don't think that will help,' David said, turning around so that Sophie could see the many pulled threads and one tiny hole.

Sophie could feel herself blush. 'I'll buy you a new one. Just let me have the details.'

'I doubt you could afford it,' David said, and his eyes strayed to Sophie's car, which was elderly in the sense that it needed lots of careful mechanical attention. 'And anyway, it was a limited edition. My girlfriend brought it for me.'

Sophie watched as David's face told her that he had been transported to another place with another person and tried to fight down the mixture of embarrassment and irritation at his manner.

'I am so, so sorry. If I can't replace it then I'll give you the money for it. Perhaps you could ask your girlfriend how much and let me know?' Inwardly, Sophie was desperately trying to work out how much money she could afford to give him, and also how much his girlfriend might have paid for such a ridiculous item of clothing.

'Forget about it,' he said gruffly, moving a discarded pizza box to uncover the bin — which was completely empty, all the rubbish in the caravan being anywhere but in the bin — and stuffing the sweater inside, before letting the lid fall back with a clang. Sophie had the distinct feeling that whatever was happening, it was not all about her or Maple, and so she decided now was a good time to excuse herself.

'If there's anything I can do to make it up to you, let me know.' The words came out in a jumble and she winced at what she had said.

She was sorry that Maple had ruined his precious jumper, but it wasn't like she had purposefully gone out of her way to damage his property. It was just a jumper, maybe an extremely expensive one but more fool him for buying it. And if it was so expensive, then why wasn't it hung up somewhere instead of thrown carelessly on the bed? As she scuttled down the steps with Maple held firmly in her arms, her guilty conscience reminded her. He hadn't bought it, of course — his girlfriend had. She felt an odd twinge at the thought that David had a girlfriend but quickly brushed it aside. She had plenty of things to focus on other than her grumpy next door neighbour, even if he was rather handsome.

Sophie closed her caravan door behind her and did a visual check to ensure all possible escape routes for Maple were closed off.

'Where did you go? I was so worried,' she murmured into Maple's fur before gently placing her in the cat bed which she had arranged in a sunny spot. 'And did you really have to find refuge with him?'

Sophie found herself scanning the next door caravan for signs of life, suddenly worried he might be able to hear her.

'I mean,' she said, turning her attention back to Maple who was sat in her upright statue position, 'I know we both have the same opinion of ridiculously expensive clothes, but was a sit-down protest really necessary?'

Sophie could have sworn Maple raised a non-existent eyebrow.

'That's not to say I'm not totally relieved that you found somewhere safe to hide out after he scared you.'

Sophie reached up to one of the small cupboards and pulled out the emergency cat treats, which sat next to the emergency bar of Belgian chocolate. She pondered whether this was a suitable time to indulge herself but resisted the temptation and shut the door. The oh-so-familiar rattle of cat treats made Maple's ears prick up and Sophie knew, for once, that she had her cat's full attention.

'He clearly is not a cat lover,' she said seriously. 'I know, I know — we're not keen on people who don't like cats, but he is our neighbour and I have to work with him, not to mention the fact that I have no friends within a two hundred mile radius, so please can we make an effort to avoid irritating him more than absolutely necessary?'

A soft paw on the hand Sophie was holding the packet in told her that lecture time was over and she needed to pay up — in cat treats. Sophie shook out a few and Maple descended on them as if she hadn't been fed for days.

Curled up in bed later, with Maple in her usual position under one arm, and a book in the other hand, Sophie felt like she was home. It had been a trying day, what with the journey and losing Maple, but she was finally here. She had been waiting to start a new chapter in her life for a long time and tomorrow it would officially begin.

'Tomorrow is the first day of the rest of our lives,' she said to Maple, tickling her behind her right ear and being rewarded with deep, comforting purrs.

As Sophie's eyes slowly closed, her mind drifted to David, and the memories of his handsome face, first exasperated, then irritated, and then . . . Then what? Sad? Angry? Or something else? Sophie wasn't sure, but she thought it must have something to do with his girlfriend. Judging by the state of his caravan, she wasn't staying with David. In fact, Sophie was pretty sure that his girlfriend wasn't due a visit anytime soon. Or maybe Sophie was just hoping she wasn't.

She quickly banished the thought. She didn't have time for distractions, and even if she did, she was pretty certain he had already made up his mind about her. Something along the lines of financially challenged, unfashionably clothed, mad cat lady, who had chosen to come back to a place he was clearly desperate to get away from.

'No distractions,' she whispered to Maple, who half opened a sleepy eye and studied Sophie briefly, before sighing out a purr and going back to sleep.

3

Sophie woke to hazy sunlight and a not-so-gentle patting paw on her nose.

'Breakfast time already?' Sophie asked, and was rewarded with a plaintive meow.

She slipped her feet out of bed and searched for her slippers. It was early May and there was definitely still a late spring chill in the air. Pulling on a jumper and doing the usual morning avoid-cat-winding-round-your-legs two-step, she clicked on the kettle and shook some dried food into Maple's food bowl. With a slightly disgruntled ripple of fur, Maple settled down to eat, clearly unhappy at the lack of tuna.

Sophie noticed a slip of white paper taped to the outside of the door window and pulled the door open curiously. It was a note from Gwen inviting her to the team meeting, which always happened at eight-thirty every Monday morning and was accompanied by a full Welsh breakfast. Sophie glanced at her watch. She had fifteen minutes and since she hated being late for anything, she grabbed her wash bag, towel and some clean clothes, warned Maple to behave, and headed to the team meeting via the showers.

The sign on the office door said 'closed', but when Sophie tried the handle it opened and she could hear the sounds of voices. One with a Welsh lilt that Sophie knew was Gwen's, and the others more distinctly English. There was no one in the main reception area, so Sophie walked past the fridge containing milk, butter and cheese and lifted the counter flap so she could get to the back room.

Several small tables had been pushed together and covered with a bright red gingham tablecloth. Jeff sat nearest to her with his plastered foot resting on a cushion on the ground. Next to him were a couple who looked to be in their fifties, who smiled up at her over their steaming mugs of coffee, and then there was David. He was slumped in his chair, paying all his attention to his phone, which occasionally let out a digital ping.

'Sophie, lass, we weren't sure you were going to make it,' Jeff said. 'After that journey yesterday we thought you might need a bit of a lie-in.'

He gestured for her to take the seat next to him. She wavered for a moment, as that would place her next to David, who clearly was not looking for any company, let alone hers.

'David!' a sharp voice sounded, clearly Welsh and clearly Gwen. 'Where are your manners?' She placed a plate in front of Jeff and then a cup of black coffee in front of David. 'Put that away! The rest of us might be used to your lack of conversation in the morning, but you could at least make an effort for Sophie's first day.'

Sophie blushed and quickly settled into the offered seat, hoping the drama would pass. With an exaggerated sigh, David made a great show of putting his phone in his back jean pocket. Sophie tried a small smile as by way of apologising for drawing his mum's attention, but it was not returned. Instead, Sophie was conscious of the waves of sulkiness that David was emanating, doing a perfectly serviceable impression of a stroppy teenager. Feeling it was a bit much — he was an adult, after all — she turned her attention away from David to the other couple, who proceeded to introduce themselves.

'You must be Sophie?' the man said. He had thick-rimmed glasses, short, greying hair and the kind of tan that only comes from working outside or excessive sunbed use.

'I'm Paul, and this lovely lady is my wife, Lydia.'

Feeling slightly shy all of a sudden, Sophie smiled and gave a little wave. David shifted in his seat next to her, giving the impression that she had somehow managed to irritate him with the simple gesture. Since ignoring rude people had been a tactic she used at school, she decided to do the same, focusing all her attention on Paul and Lydia.

Paul had launched into an extended monologue about how he and Lydia had ended up working on the site and had just moved onto the subject of grandchildren, of which they had an astonishing twelve, when Lydia gave him a sharp elbow in the ribs. Clearly he was well used to this signal, as he stopped talking, his voice drifting off mid-sentence on the subject of Matthew, their eldest. Lydia looked at Sophie with twinkling eyes.

'Sorry about that, love. My Paul can go on when you get him onto one of his favourite subjects!'

She grinned at her husband and he returned it, before taking a sip of his coffee.

'He seems to think he's only got one breath to tell you everything there is to know about us Taylors.'

Lydia reached over and squeezed Paul's hand. 'We've got all season, love, and I doubt Sophie really needs to know that our Matthew's a sound football player with turning professional a real possibility.'

The polite part of Sophie's brain was posed ready to make appropriately impressed noises — she was not a football fan herself but she could still understand why they were so proud, and she could see that Paul was itching to wax lyrical about his talented grandson — but David had shifted in his chair, so slumped now that even a tiny movement would have left him sitting on the floor. Sophie took that as a sign. Any encouragement on her part would be seen as yet another failure in David's eyes, and whilst she did not like being bullied she also wanted, or maybe even needed, to get on with him. Instead, she smiled at Paul in what she hoped was a 'maybe you can tell me later' kind of way, and tucked into the full Welsh breakfast that Gwen had placed in front of her.

Once the breakfast things had been cleared away — Sophie had not been allowed to help, with the general consensus being that she should sit down and relax this time — Jeff produced a printed spreadsheet.

'I put this up in reception, Sophie,' he said, passing it to her. 'That way, you know what jobs are yours on what day.'

Gwen settled in the seat opposite him, at the head of the table.

'But as it's your first week, we've put you and David down together, just so you can find your feet. Took David longer, but I'm minded that you're a bit more enthusiastic about things than he is.'

Sophie was not unaware of the mild warning look that passed between Jeff and his wife, or the fact that Lydia and Paul were now making serious studies of the flower pattern on their coffee mugs. She felt a slightly guilty twinge of relief. Perhaps David didn't have a particular problem with her. It seemed more like he had a problem with everything at Saint Peulan. She felt better that it might not be personal, but it still had the makings of a long first week if he was going to be grumpy and monosyllabic. She took another sip of tea whilst her brain formulated the plan. It would be best to get to grips with everything as soon as possible so that she could get on and do her assigned jobs by herself, preferably before the end of this week.

Sophie, dressed in her jeans and new Saint Peulan campsite T-shirt, easily kept pace with David, who seemed, if anything, to be dragging his feet. It appeared to Sophie that her workmate had transformed from stroppy teenager to truculent toddler. She had no idea what his problem was, but she really wanted to know. Her sister Helen, five years older and married with two kids, would always scold her for trying to fix other people. Helen was always quick to point out that, more often than not, people didn't want fixing. Moreover, they were aware of their problems and if they really wanted to, they would fix them themselves. An image of her sister, with hands on her hips, ready to give her another lecture, made her smile. She was probably right. Sophie had enough on her plate without trying to get to the bottom of David's issues.

'Does the prospect of cleaning twenty toilets usually make you smile?'

David's voice cut through the vision of her sister and she realised he was standing in front of her offering a pair of yellow rubber gloves and a toilet brush. Sophie rearranged her features, banishing the smile and trying to appear workman-like.

'All part of the job, I guess,' she said, taking ownership of the gloves and brush. For his part, David stared at her as if she were mad. He appeared to have lost the power of speech and so, with no further instructions forthcoming, Sophie took control of the cleaning trolley and pushed it towards the ladies.

She turned at the door, using her bottom to push it open so she could pull the trolley after her. She couldn't help risking a glance in David's direction and instantly wished she hadn't. David was still staring at her, and not in a 'you're amazing' kind of way; it was more of a 'what alien planet did you come from?' kind of way. He seemed to notice that she had turned around and it appeared to jolt him back to the here and now.

'Don't forget to put out the wet floor sign,' he said in a flat monotone.

'Of course,' she said with a smile. 'It's all about Health and Safety these days, isn't it?'

She watched as he shook his head and disappeared around the shower block, presumably to start work on the gents.

Sophie felt her heart sink just a little more, and she wondered if David's black mood might be catching. After all, it wasn't as if toilet cleaner was high on her list of most-wished-for jobs but it was a means to an end. Her dad had always said a job was a job and if someone was paying you for it then you jolly well did it to the best of your ability.

Sophie was on the third toilet cubicle when she heard the voices. Whoever they belonged to must be standing outside of the long, low window that she had propped open. Sophie could make out all their words.

'Well, me mam asked that woman in reception and she said he had some high-flying job in London.'

This news was greeted by a gasp and an 'Ohhh' noise. Sophie couldn't see them from where she was crouched, wiping a damp cloth over the toilet seat, but she could picture them in her mind's eye. It took her back to a place she had no wish to go — her old school.

'Maybe he's a doctor?' another voice said.

'Don't be daft! What would a doctor be doing working in a dump like this!'

There was the sound of sniggering,

not unlike witches at a cauldron.

'Maybe he's a lawyer then,' came the slightly hurt-sounding reply.

'Too handsome to be a solicitor.' This time the words came as if the speaker's lips were slightly open. Sophie guessed they were putting on lipstick. She smiled as she replaced the empty toilet roll with a new one. Since when did solicitors have to be ugly? Oh, the opinions of teenagers!

'I reckon he was in finance, you know, one of them stockbrokers. Probably rolling in it.' This seemed to come from the leader of the little pack.

'Then why would he be here? He should be off in the Bahamas, not cleaning the loos!'

More giggles and Sophie was now sure she knew who they were talking about.

'Maybe he spent all his money. If his mum and dad own this place, they'd put him up wouldn't they?'

'Well if he's skint, I'm not interested anyway.'

Sophie heard the unmistakable sound of flip-flops.

'There's no way I'd date someone who cleans toilets for a living!'

At this moment Sophie stepped out of the cubicle she was cleaning and was rewarded with one scathing expression and two surprised ones from the three teenagers who had just walked through the main door, ignoring the 'closed for cleaning' sign.

'But he's sooo dreamy!' one of the girls said as they all turned their attention away from Sophie.

'I'll give you that, but what use is he if he can't afford to buy you anything or take you places?' The girl with the scathing expression paused at the door. 'I mean, do you really want to do this for a living?'

The girl made a gesture to indicate her disgust and Sophie met her gaze without embarrassment. She'd had plenty of practice at school. Seeing she wasn't getting any reaction from Sophie, the girl clicked her tongue and stepped outside, the other two following like sheep. Sophie smiled. Teenagers really thought they had the whole world sorted out. She wondered what David would make of his pack of teenage admirers. Perhaps a spot of teasing might get him to lighten up a bit? An image of his sullen face at breakfast swam before her mind's eye.

'Probably not,' she said aloud to the empty bathroom, 'but I still wouldn't mind finding out exactly what is going on with him.'

As Sophie was mopping the last bit of floor near the showers she made up her mind. She was going to try and find out a bit more about him. Maybe just ask what he did before he came here. She had to admit she was intrigued — her mum would say nosy — but she couldn't spend the whole season just knowing that his name was David, he had expensive taste in clothes and didn't like cats. Her mind was made up, she'd ask him and while she was at it, maybe she would tell him a bit about her plans. Perhaps if he knew more about why she was in Wales, working at a campsite, he would stop looking at her like she was crazy. Not that she was worried about what he thought, of course. She loved the campsite and the surrounding area and she was excited to be here. And maybe, just maybe, she could get him to change his mind about the place too?

4

Considering David was supposed to be showing her the ropes, he managed to contrive a whole range of activities that they could easily achieve apart. Sophie wondered if he was able to read her mind. Did he know that she planned to find out more about him or did he simply want to be alone with his misery? If it was the latter this just made her more determined. Surely if he had to be here, which to all appearances he did, he would rather be having a bit of fun too?

Finally, mid-afternoon, Sophie thought she might have found her opportunity. David was hosing down one of the static caravans, which were available to rent, whilst Sophie used a bucket and scrubbing brush to wash off the steps and airing rack. Making sure that David was looking the other way, she quickly stepped into the line of water so that she was lightly sprayed.

'Oi!' she shouted in mock indignation. He glanced at her in such a distracted way that she felt sure his mind had been firmly fixed elsewhere. His eyes glided over the line of splashes that ran from the bottom of Sophie's T-shirt down the front of her jeans, his stare unnerving her just a little.

'Did you do that on purpose?' she said, keeping her voice light and mischievous so he would be in no doubt that she was joking.

'Of course not,' he said grumpily, before yanking hard on the hose and stalking off to next caravan.

She watched the tightness in his shoulders and couldn't ignore the unhappiness that seemed to ooze from him. Clearly something was very wrong, something personal and obviously painful. Now was clearly not the time to ask him what it was. He wasn't going to tell her in his current mood but maybe she could distract him a little? Force him to let go and have a little fun. Ignoring her sister's warning voice in her head, telling her it was a bad idea, she picked up the sponge and soaked it in her bucket, in deference to her poor throwing ability she squeezed out a little of the water and then snuck around the back of the next door van. David had his back to her and she could tell that once again he had retreated to his unhappy place.

'David?' she called innocently.

With a slight sag of his shoulders he turned around and was rewarded with a wet car sponge in his face. Some of the soap stuck to his eyebrows and his hair, giving him the air of a younger Boris Johnson. Sophie's giggle died on her lips and she had to swallow the lump that had suddenly appeared in her throat. His expression was frozen, in anger. With a furious hand he wiped away the soap suds from his face as if she had thrown something foul and smelly at him. He glared at her.

Sophie had thought he might splutter

a bit and then pretend to be mad at her, and possibly spray her from head to toe with cold water at worst, but there was no escaping how genuinely angry he was.

'Sorry, I, er, thought it might lighten the mood . . . ' The words died on her lips. Without intending to, she had made things a thousand times worse.

'I'm going to change,' he said coldly, picking at his T-shirt which was, in fact, much drier than her own. 'Can I take it you can manage this last van on your own?' His voice had gone from cold to arctic.

'Of course.' Sophie felt flustered. 'I'm sorry . . . '

David had clearly decided that the best approach was to ignore her, as he turned on his heel and stalked away, waving a hand imperiously in response to her second attempt to apologise. Now it was Sophie's turn to stare. She didn't think she had ever met someone with quite such a sense of humour failure. Perhaps something really tragic had happened to him and his misery was in fact inconsolable grief? She thought of Jeff and Gwen, who had not shown any signs of sorrow other than concern for their son, so it seemed unlikely it was a family bereavement. Sophie's mind wandered as she picked up her sponge and bucket and began to scrub the winter grime off another set of steps.

An image of the pink jumper, incredibly soft and ridiculously expensive, swam before her eyes. David had been so upset to find that Maple had nested on it. At the time she had assumed it was because it was so expensive, but now that she thought about it, she was sure that she was wrong. It was clearly valuable to him, but perhaps she had misjudged him? Perhaps its value was sentimental. David had said his girlfriend had given it to him. He had seemed so reluctant to disclose its value, but maybe he had no way of finding out.

By the time she had finished hosing

down the back of the caravan, Sophie had convinced herself that she had solved the mystery that was David. His girlfriend had clearly died in tragic circumstances. She couldn't help but mentally tell herself off. How could she have been so insensitive? In fact, she prided herself in being good at telling when something was wrong. David didn't need jollying up. He needed space and understanding. She pushed away the guilt. It wasn't as if she could change anything that had happened, but she could change how she was with him from now on. She would be quietly supportive and helpful and then maybe at some point in the future they might become friends and she might be able to fix some of the damage she had done.

For the rest of the afternoon, Sophie worked silently by David's side. She no longer asked questions in the hope of striking up a conversation; instead, she spoke only when she really needed to. For his part, David seemed to relax a little. As far as Sophie was concerned, this was more evidence that her theory was correct.

Sophie walked back from the showers, one hand to her aching neck. The day had not started well, but it had definitely improved. Sophie liked to have a plan and now she had one for dealing with David. It was very early days, of course, but all the signs from the afternoon were promising.

She unlocked the door to her new home, thinking that she really ought to venture out to the local supermarket but knowing that what she really wanted was a cup of tea and to curl up on the sofa with Maple and her book. She scanned the main room of the caravan, which comprised the kitchen, dining and living room and could spot no sign of Maple. Sophie wasn't overly concerned; she expected that Maple would be curled up on her bed, in her favourite spot on the patchwork quilt her mum had made her. But there was no Maple. Sophie pushed down the feeling of panic. There were quite a few good hiding places. She began to search.

Sophie knew she should have double-checked all the escape routes, but the morning had been a rush and she had thought Maple would be happy just to sleep all day, as was her usual routine. Sophie walked to the back window to check out the surrounding grass and wooded area, but there was nothing. With a sigh that was a cross between concern and parent-like frustration, she threw herself down on the sofa. And that was when she saw her. Maple, smug as you like, sunbathing in the late afternoon sun on David's sofa, in David's caravan.

5

Sophie just stared. This could not be happening again! She couldn't help but think that any repair to her fledgling friendship with David was about to be wiped out by one small, furry feline.

Although Maple was sat directly on the sofa, with no expensive cashmere sweater in sight, Sophie groaned, wondering what damage her delinquent cat might have caused. She scanned the area and sighed with relief when she could see no signs of David. Hoping his delay would give her enough time, she started to tap furiously on the inside of her window, hoping to get Maple's attention. Whether Maple couldn't hear her or couldn't be bothered to acknowledge her, Sophie wasn't sure. Cats could be fickle that way. She used her feet to find her trainers, forcing them on without bothering to untie the laces, keeping her eyes fixed on the park beyond David's static caravan and hoping that whatever had kept him away from his home would keep him away a little longer.

Sophie stepped outside her van and quietly closed the door. She took one last peek around David's van and then quickly ran to his side window. Since the caravan was held off the ground by a set of breeze blocks, Sophie couldn't actually see into the van, but could just about make out some black fur, squished against the window. Using her fingernails Sophie tapped lightly on the window. The smudge of black fur that she could see didn't so much as ruffle. She could feel herself getting more cross, and flushed with embarrassment. How could this be happening, again?

Sophie searched around and her eyes settled on a set of metal steps which she hurried to collect and dumped underneath the window. She made a fist, glanced over her shoulder for any sign of David, took a deep breath and then hammered on the window. This time Sophie saw Maple's fur ripple, probably with irritation, but no actual movement from her pet. Sophie stepped up on to the top step so that she was now on a direct eye level with Maple.

'Maple!' she hissed through clenched teeth. 'What are you doing in there? We talked about this!'

Maple sat up slowly, flicked her tail and blinked at Sophie. Sophie started to make hand gestures indicating that Maple needed to leave now, before David came home but Maple simply lifted a front paw and began to casually wash it. In total exasperation Sophie started to hammer on the window, hard, hoping that might startle Maple enough to make her move. And that was when the window opened.

The caramel-coloured hair was even more ruffled than usual, sticking up on one side and plastered to his head on the other. David's face seemed almost blurry and Sophie's heart sank when she realised she had woken him up.

David looked from the cat to Sophie and back again. Maple, for her part, stretched out her back and padded towards David before head-butting his shoulder. David seemed to freeze and Sophie opened her mouth to begin apologising when Maple lifted a paw placing it carefully on David's chin and looking him sorrowfully in the eyes.

Sophie murmured 'Sorry,' although she knew that David would not be able to hear her, jumped off the top step and dashed around to the van door. Here, she paused, wondering whether she should knock. Feeling slightly foolish, she rapped on the door lightly and then pushed it open. Stepping over a pair of discarded trainers and what she could only assume was a pile of clothes waiting to visit a washing machine, she made her way to the seating area at the back of the van. What she saw was not what she was expecting.

David was laid back down, his head on a cushion with his eyes closed and Maple was tucked under his chin.

David appeared to have surrendered to Maple's demands and was gently stroking her ears. Sophie stood there, not knowing what to do next. Should she grab her cat and run or leave the pair to it? They seemed perfectly comfortable. David opened one eye.

'Relax, Sophie. It seems your cat's persistence has won me over.'

'I'm so sorry. I've no idea how she got out of my van, let alone into yours.' Sophie knew she was wringing her hands but couldn't seem to stop.

'I left all my windows open,' David said, his voice even and unconcerned. 'And besides, I only had one cashmere sweater.'

Sophie's attention quickly moved from her traitor cat to David's face. She felt the tension melt from her shoulders when she saw his face break into a smile. He opened his eyes again and Sophie saw a little light dance in them, which was a first.

'She can stay here with me if you have things to do.' David's voice had a casual air but Sophie wasn't fooled. Maple, it seemed, had worked her feline wiles on him and he was yet another conquest.

'Actually, I was going to go and get a few supplies. If you're sure you don't mind?' Sophie could feel her lips twitch as she tried not to smile.

'I think I can cope,' he said without opening his eyes, clearly in the zone.

'Do you need anything?' Sophie asked, not bothering to hide her smile as Maple turned her face to her looking triumphant.

'Pepperoni pizza and a couple of bottles of beer?'

'Sure. I won't be long,' Sophie said, not even sure he'd heard her, and she made her way out of the caravan, marvelling at how her cat had won David over, when she seemed unable to.

★ ★ ★

Sophie dumped her bags of shopping on the floor. She quickly searched through them and found everything that needed cold storage and shoved the packets haphazardly into the fridge and tiny freezer compartment. Although it went against all her personal tidiness rules, she decided to leave the rest of the shopping in the bags until after she had collected Maple. She didn't want to push her luck with David and Maple's burgeoning friendship, which she felt could turn sour at any moment. Grabbing the pizza and the beer, she made her way to David's van. Pushing open the door, this time without knocking, she could hear scrabbling and had a sudden vision of Maple clawing at the material of David's sofa.

'Maple!' she said firmly. 'Stop that at once!'

The two in front of her froze like a tableau, both looked a little guilty. David was holding a piece of string that he had attached a balled-up sock to, and Maple was mid-grab, claws ready to catch it as it swung back. Maple was the first to move, making a four-legged leap across David's lap to where the homemade cat toy had come to rest. This time Sophie didn't bother to hide her grin.

'Well, I'm glad to see you're both enjoying yourselves,' she said, putting the beer and pizza on the only free surface space in the kitchenette.

David pulled the balled-up sock on the floor and once he was sure he had Maple's attention, he yanked it away so that she performed a kind of half somersault. Sophie clapped, unable to restrain herself. David made a sort of half bow and Sophie noticed the glimmer of a smile again.

'Thanks for cat-sitting and entertaining her. It's nice to see you both getting on,' Sophie couldn't help adding. She noticed an emotion cross David's face like a cloud momentarily blocking out the sun. One moment it was there and then it was gone. To Sophie it spoke of deep sadness that David was once again forcing down. She felt the urge to ask but ignored it.

'Enjoy your supper, and thanks again for watching Maple.'

Sophie carefully navigated her way to the door. She made soft clicking noises with her tongue which occasionally worked on Maple.

'Stay?'

The word made Sophie freeze and for a moment she was sure she had imagined it. She risked a glance in his direction and saw that he was looking at her closely.

'There's plenty of pizza, and my mum is always saying that drinking alone isn't healthy.' David gestured at the four bottles of beer that Sophie had left on the side.

Sophie studied his face, wondering if the invite was genuine or if he had been pressganged into it by Gwen, but she saw only a look of honesty on his face. Sophie opened her mouth to speak at the same time that Maple meowed pitifully, obviously hungry.

'Er . . . ' Sophie said, wondering whether this was a good excuse to go, but at the same time not sure that she wanted to. Despite his teenage sulkiness, Sophie suspected that there was a decent man underneath, and if her suspicions as to his tragic past were correct then he deserved a second chance.

'I have some ham in the fridge and a sausage mum gave me that was left over at breakfast.' He frowned momentarily. 'She seems to think if she doesn't give me leftovers I won't eat.' He looked up at her and clocked her expression. 'For Maple, of course. I mean, I'm guessing her protests are because her belly's empty?'

Sophie didn't have to answer him as, just as if she had understood every word of the conversation, Maple had started to wind herself around his leg and then proceeded to nip at his toes. Sophie tensed but David just smiled distractedly and leant down to stoke her.

'If Maple's up for it, then so am I.'

Sophie couldn't work out why, but all

of a sudden she felt shy and there was another feeling she couldn't pinpoint. Perhaps it was because she knew she couldn't afford to be distracted by anything, let alone a handsome man next door. Particularly one who was in the depths of despair and grief. And not for the obvious reasons. She wanted to be his friend but she knew from bitter experience what it was like to be the rebound girl. She mentally shook herself; it was just pizza and a beer. She had to work with David and live next door; it would be nice to get to know him as a friend.

'You okay?' David asked and Sophie saw a look of concern on his face, which was a new experience.

'Just thinking,' she said hurriedly. 'About the future, you know; things like that.' Sophie turned away momentarily and hoped that her usual open-book face hadn't given her away.

David nodded and reached across her to turn on the small oven, waiting for the click that told them the gas was lit. 'Do you want a glass or is straight from the bottle okay?'

Sophie's eyes were somehow drawn to the many dirty glasses that littered every surface, including the floor. 'Bottle's fine,' she said, taking it from his out stretched hand.

'Good answer,' he said. 'If you'd have said yes, I'm afraid I would have had to go wash up.'

Sophie returned his smile as he pulled a bottle opener out of the Swiss Army knife that he kept on his belt. With one hand covering hers, he used the bottle opener to pop off the cap with a hiss. Sophie barely noticed, as all her attention was on the feel of his hand on hers. It was only when she heard a second hiss that she registered his hand was gone. Glancing up at him, she knew that whatever she had felt in that moment was not shared, and she forced herself to shrug off the sensation, whilst firmly reminding herself what had happened last time.

David gestured for her to take a seat,

which she did, with one leg curled up underneath her. She watched as he cut up the ham and sausage for Maple. Maple, for her part, stretched up her front paws to the hips of his trousers and sniffed the air with anticipation. David went to put the plate on the floor and Maple nearly nudged it out of his hands.

'Careful, puss,' he said, before gently tickling her ear. David checked the light on the oven before unwrapping the pizza and placing it inside.

'So,' he said, taking a swig from his beer and settling himself on the other side of the table that sat in the middle of the 'U' of sofa seats, 'why exactly are you here?'

6

Sophie took a sip of beer to give herself a few moments to consider her answer and looked down, hoping to hide the flaming colour in her cheeks.

'You know that I would literally rather be any place else, but you seem glad.'

'It's a long story,' Sophie said finally, wondering how to word it so she didn't sound like a complete wet blanket.

'I'm listening and besides there's not a whole lot else to do out here in the middle of deepest, darkest Wales.'

Sophie was still trying to figure out where to start, but David seemed to interpret this as reluctance to tell her story.

'You may not have noticed yet, but the TV signal's appalling.'

Sophie looked up and saw a genuine smile, which had seemed such an impossibility even this morning.

'Okay,' she said, taking a deep breath. 'But you have to promise not to judge.'

David raised his beer. 'Trust me, Sophie. I'm in no place to judge anyone.'

Sophie watched him for a couple of heartbeats, wondering again if her instinct was right, that he had suffered some deep, personal tragedy like the death of his girlfriend. Perhaps if she told him about her experiences he would open up about his own.

'I had this boyfriend in college.' Sophie couldn't help herself, she had to watch him closely for a reaction. Most people at this point rolled their eyes. 'I really loved him, and I thought he loved me.'

David nodded to show he was listening but made no comment, just smoothed down Maple's ears as she wound her way across the sofa.

'Anyway, we were all set to go to Uni. We both had the grades and we were going to the same place. But the summer before I was due to go, my nephew Aiden got really sick. My sister had just had another baby and my mum already cares for my dad, who's disabled, so I knew what I needed to do.'

Sophie gripped the bottle of beer. She had never regretted the decision she had made. She had always known it was the right one, but the consequences of that decision remained painful however much she pretended that she had moved on.

'You didn't go to Uni?' David asked quietly and now Sophie realised he was studying her.

'I couldn't really. I mean, it was completely my own decision. Everyone told me I had to go, but some things in life are more important.' Sophie froze and winced, knowing that her last comment might sound like she was judging David, but he merely shrugged and gestured for her to continue.

'Aiden was only three. Jessica just a couple of months. In the beginning, the doctors weren't sure whether Aiden would, you know . . . ' Sophie paused as she swallowed the lump in her throat. 'So I moved in with my sister and brother-in-law and did whatever I could to help out.'

'So no Uni?' David asked

'Actually yes,' Sophie said with a smile. 'I signed up to a distance learning course. It took me five years, but I got my degree, eventually.'

'Wow,' David said, looking impressed. 'And how's Aiden?'

There was that expression on his face that everyone had when they were asking about how a sick child was. It was a look of concern mixed with perhaps the desire not to know if it was bad news.

'He's good. Seven operations and more stays in hospital than at home, but he's doing alright.' She smiled at the memory of Aiden, charging round the garden with his dad, chasing a football, something that they all thought they would never get to see again. 'He'll probably need another couple of operations as he grows, but he's finally out of danger.'

'That's great,' David said as his watch beeped. Sophie allowed the silence to sit as she watched him get the pizza out of the oven and then hunt for the pizza cutter. Eventually, under an old newspaper, he found it. Sophie wasn't entirely convinced it was clean, but decided to ignore that fact. With no clean plates to be found, David placed the pizza into the torn off lid of its box and placed it on the table, where it balanced precariously on piles of stuff.

'Not the best housekeeper,' David said, and for the first time he actually looked sheepish at the state of his home.

'Pizza's hot, that's all that matters. I'm starving,' Sophie said as she reached out for a slice.

'So what happened with the college boyfriend?' David said, tucking into his second slice and lounging back on the sofa so that Maple could settle next to him.

'That's another long story.' Sophie sighed at the memory. 'But essentially, he said that he understood why I had to stay. Promised he would come home and visit me lots, and then met someone new in Freshers' Week.'

'Ouch,' David said, which made Sophie giggle.

'It has all the hallmarks of a tragic romance really. He didn't tell me until the end of the first term, but I knew him, I knew something was going on. He dated Stephanie until his last year and then she dumped him.'

Sophie couldn't help it, a mischievous smile crossed her lips and she knew David had seen it.

'Sounds like he deserved that one.'

'Unfortunately, that's not where the story ends. He came home that Christmas and begged for forgiveness. He told me I was his one true love and that he'd behaved like an idiot.'

Sophie grimaced as a vision of a

tearful Steve swam in front of her eyes.

'Ah. And I take it you believed him,' David said gently.

'Yep. Like a total fool. I bought it. I still loved him, even after all the lying and all the other stunts he pulled. Then he dumped me again by text, a few weeks after declaring I was his soul mate.'

David nearly choked on his beer.

'What a jerk,' he said with feeling, and Sophie smiled.

'Yeah, he was, but I was foolish enough to fall for it.'

'I don't think trusting the person you love is foolish,' David said, and when Sophie looked at him he was looking out into the darkness beyond the caravan's windows.

'Maybe, but that's not how it felt at the time, or now, three years after the fact.'

'Sounds like you had your heart broken. That's not something that heals quickly.'

Sophie raised an eyebrow in surprise.

Somehow, she wasn't used to comments like that from a man, and she was certain now that they shared a common experience. But who had broken his heart, and how? For a few minutes they sat in silence, but it was the companionable kind. It felt in that moment as if she and David were old friends. She watched as he tickled Maple's ears, lost in thought.

'I know you have a story too,' Sophie said softly. 'No pressure to share, but I'm a pretty good listener if you ever want to.'

David turned his attention back to her and his expression registered surprise, as if he had suddenly remembered that she was still here.

'Thanks,' he said at last, and Sophie could see the effort in his face as he struggled with emotions that had come to the surface. 'Maybe another time. And besides, you haven't finished yours.'

Sophie frowned. 'That's pretty much it.'

David smiled. 'You've told me your tragic love story.' Sophie looked up sharply, but there was no jesting in his eyes, instead, they showed understanding. 'But you still haven't told me why you've chosen a self-imposed banishment to the backwaters of Wales.'

He laughed now, and Sophie shook her head in mock anger.

'Firstly, it's a beautiful part of the world . . . ' David raised his eyebrows in an 'if you say so' gesture. 'And secondly, I'm here to follow my dreams.'

'Now this, I have got to hear,' he said, standing up carefully so as not to disturb Maple. 'Another beer?'

7

'I've always wanted to be a teacher.'

David nodded.

'What?' Sophie asked, torn between curious and amused.

'I can see you as a teacher, and you certainly have the teacher voice down pat. I knew I was in serious trouble when I opened your car door and the moglet escaped.'

Now Sophie did laugh. She had never really thought about it before, but maybe David was right. She had spent enough time around children, helping out as a reader at Aiden's school, that she had had some practice.

'I suppose I have, but hopefully I'm not that scary.'

'I'm guessing your average eight-year-old is used to it but as for us twenty-six-year-olds, you were pretty scary.'

Sophie elbowed him now and he rolled away in mock pain.

'I don't think you're allowed to do that in the classroom. However much they annoy you.'

Sophie flashed her eyes at him, another technique she had learned, but this one from her sister.

'Okay, okay,' David said, holding his hands up in surrender. 'I totally get the wanting to be a teacher bit. I'm just not sure why you felt the need to come to this backwater to do it.'

Sophie shook her head.

'I really don't get why you seem to hate it so much, but maybe that's another story.' Sophie paused, but it quickly became clear that David wasn't ready to talk about himself. 'I spent almost every summer here as a child and I loved it!'

'What did you do all day?'

'We played in the woods, built forts, we had a whole new set of friends every week as new people came and went. We had sports tournaments and board game tournaments.'

'Board game tournaments?' David asked, incredulously.

'Don't knock it till you try it.'

David did not look convinced.

'Each day one of you picks a game and challenges the others. The score board runs for the whole summer and at the end someone is crowned the winner.'

'Well you certainly know how to party.'

Sophie could feel herself blush. She always felt like she was out of step with others her age.

'I'm only teasing,' David said with a look of concern. 'Since there isn't much else to do round here of an evening, why don't we resurrect your grand tradition?'

Sophie watched for the tell-tale signs that she was being set up for a fall, as she had been when she was enthusiastic about anything at school.

'I'm serious,' David said. 'Before you arrived, I was literally down to watching the soaps with my folks. Anything has to be better than that depressing nonsense.'

David stood up and flicked the switch on the coffee.

'And since it's your idea, you can pick first.'

'Okay, my van tomorrow evening. I'll make dinner, you bring wine.'

'Coffee?' David said, and the smile that Sophie had thought so elusive when she first met him, reappeared.

'I'm assuming that wasn't the only reason?' David asked, as Sophie nursed her coffee cup.

'Nope,' Sophie said, looking up at him. 'It came down to the finances in the end. My grandparents were both Welsh and so I spoke Welsh in the holidays. There's a shortage of Welsh-speaking teachers and so they're offering a small bursary and will pay my fees.' Sophie took a sip of her coffee. 'I haven't had much chance to save up, what with everything going on at home, and this meant I could start this September. I've waited so long I didn't want to wait any longer.'

Sophie was aware that David was staring at her.

'What?' she asked again, feeling like another person was going to tell her how crazy her plan was, especially since he hadn't heard about the crucial issue yet.

'Nothing,' he said, shaking his head. 'Actually, that's not true. I was thinking about how focused you've been on what you want from life, even when it's thrown you a curveball.' He looked thoughtful. 'I have to say, I'm impressed.'

Now Sophie experienced a full blush, one that started in her neck and ended with her cheeks turning scarlet. She was so used to having to defend her decisions, used to the incredulous expressions and the sense that everyone thought she had gone completely mad. Then the elephant in the room reared its trunk again

'I'm not sure you should be.'

David opened his mouth to speak but seeing Sophie's expression, the words didn't make it out.

'There is one slight problem.'

'Don't tell me — you can't remember how to speak Welsh.'

Sophie winced and watched David's eyes go wide. It took him a moment to process it and then he was laughing, proper hold-your-sides laughing. Sophie was feeling a little disconcerted; no one had ever reacted like this.

'I know, I know,' she said, flapping her hands. 'It's not that I can't speak it exactly. It's just that I never learned to read or write it.'

Once again the cold spot in Sophie's stomach seemed to grow. Everyone else was right. She was mad, quite mad. To think that she could teach herself to both read and write Welsh in three months whilst holding down her job in the caravan park was insane.

'You are priceless,' David said, clearly making an effort to compose himself.

'What are you going to do? I mean, I think they'll notice.'

'The interview was over the phone, so all I had to do was talk in Welsh. I've brought a couple of books and I'm going to teach myself this summer.'

She wasn't sure who she was trying to convince, herself or David.

'Teach yourself?' David asked, and now his face was looking a lot more serious than it had a few moments before.

'People do it all the time,' Sophie said in what she hoped was an airy tone.

'French and Spanish, maybe but I'm not so sure about Welsh. It's not the easiest to learn.'

Sophie sagged. She knew he was right. What she was going to have to do was find someone to tutor her, but she had no idea how she was going to afford that. She mulled over what David had said.

'How do you know it's hard to learn?' she asked.

'I went to school in Wales, and in

north Wales it's mandatory.'

He smiled a little. Sophie knew this of course, as that was why she was here.

'But you don't sound Welsh,' she said, as it was the only thing she could think of to say.

'Thank you,' he said as if Sophie had offered him some great compliment. 'We moved to Wales when I was five and everyone at school took the mickey out of my posh English accent. Mum had always spoken in Welsh to us at home so I could speak the language but I sounded different so I worked to get the accent too. When I was sixteen we moved back to Lancashire and then the opposite happened, so I worked hard to lose it again.'

Sophie leant back on the sofa. That, she thought, did explain a few things.

'I can help you, if you like,' David said.

Now it was Sophie's turn to go wide-eyed.

'You can still write and read Welsh?'

Sophie couldn't believe it.

'Yes,' he said with a rather self-important smile. 'In my job in London, I worked with the firm's Welsh clients. So I've kept my hand in, so to speak.'

Sophie felt as if the cold spot in her stomach had suddenly been microwaved. The relief was so powerful that she found herself throwing her arms around David's neck.

'Thank you, thank you,' she squealed, and then, realising that he was not returning the hug with quite the same level of enthusiasm, she drew away.

'Sorry,' she said, mentally reminding herself of what he had been through. 'It's just I've been so worried about this. If you could help me out, even a little, that would be fantastic.'

David seemed to find his smile again.

'If you don't mind putting up with my mood swings, then the least I can do is help you out a bit.'

Sophie smiled in what she hoped was an encouraging but not pushy way.

'Okay, and if you help me with my Welsh, why don't I help you out with . . . '

Sophie's eyes scanned the van, which looked like it hadn't been tidied up in at least a year.

'Oh, no!' David said, holding his hands up. 'Not you, too. My mum is itching to get in here and 'sort out', as she puts it.' David made quotation marks with his fingers. 'I don't need anyone to clean up after me. It's messy, but it's my mess and I'm happy with it.'

'Well there must be something,' Sophie said, knowing that she couldn't accept his offer, however badly she needed his help, without doing something in return.

'Look,' David said, running a hand through his hair and ruffling it, 'to be honest, just having someone my age to hang out with, have a beer with, that's kind of all I need right now.'

Sophie could tell that David needed more than that. He needed someone to listen and to understand. He wasn't able to say those words out loud, but she was sure of it.

'Of course, although I'm not sure you're getting a very good deal out of this.'

David turned and looked at her, really looked at her, for what felt like the first time. There was a message in his brown eyes but she couldn't decipher it.

'Trust me; I'd be happy with that.'

Sophie nodded slowly, wondering if he would say more, but he didn't. Instead, he stood up. Glancing at her watch, she realised how late it was.

'I'd better be going,' she said hurriedly. 'It's late. I'm sorry for talking for so long.'

'It makes a change to listen to someone other than myself,' he said, scooping up Maple and handing the sleepy cat over to her.

'Thanks,' she said, 'for everything. Do you want to come over for dinner about seven tomorrow?'

'Okay, but how about I get to you for six? Then we can do an hour of Welsh before we eat.'

Sophie was more than a little surprised by his seeming enthusiasm to spend time with her. That small part of her brain that she kept closely guarded was starting to go into overdrive. 'It's because he likes you,' the little voice said. She felt a fizz of excitement rush through her, but she firmly pushed it back. She didn't have time for romance and she was sure that David was not emotionally ready for another relationship. You didn't just get over the death of your other half in a few months, the sensible part of her brain butted in. Realising she was standing in the middle of his caravan having a mental argument with herself, whilst he looked on curiously, she mumbled, 'Good night,' and dashed next door. She could continue her internal dialogue in the safety of her own van, without an audience.

8

Sophie had set her alarm half an hour earlier than normal so that she could make a spaghetti bolognese for dinner. It had been a week since her first day and she was getting back into the routine of camping life. Cooking dinner in the morning meant she would have half an hour or so before David arrived to practise her Welsh, and she needed it. It was slow going, although David had proved to be a surprisingly patient teacher. He had been modest about his Welsh too; he was clearly very fluent. In the half hour before he arrived, she would feel the panic rising — she just knew she would not be ready to start in September. She already knew there were full assessments of writing and reading Welsh in that first week, and she couldn't imagine she would be allowed to stay if she failed them miserably.

Then David would arrive, and the panic would start to fade. She told herself firmly this was just because he was such a good teacher, but a small part of her brain warned her that she was starting to fall for him.

She forced that part of her back into its cupboard and firmly closed the door. She didn't have time for romance, and if she was honest, she wasn't ready to risk her heart again. What she hadn't told David was how long it had taken her to get over Steve. He was the real reason her dreams had been on hold for so long. It felt like she had let him steal three years of her life, and she wasn't ready to let someone else in who might do the same. Besides, although David still rarely spoke about himself and never about his past, he was clearly not ready for a relationship either.

Maple, licking the last remnants of her breakfast from her lips, started howling at the door. It seemed Sophie wasn't the only one who enjoyed spending time with David. She opened the caravan door and watched as Maple trotted, tail in its usual question mark, across the space between the two vans. As if they had some kind of psychic connection, Sophie heard the door to David's van open and close and could hear the two friends greet each other.

Sophie ignored the twinge of jealousy she felt and went back to chopping onions whilst trying to translate a paragraph of Welsh into English. She finished cooking dinner, then there was a knock at the door and she grabbed her sweatshirt as she opened it.

'Maple is settled at mine so I've left the window open,' David said, greeting her with a smile that Sophie had decided suited him far more than the scowl he had been wearing.

'How's the translation going?' he asked, as he stepped backwards so that Sophie could lock her caravan door.

'How did you know?' she asked with a frown.

David laughed.

'You are the most dedicated student

I've ever had,' he answered in Welsh.

'I'm the only student you've ever had,' she answered back.

David had suggested that she should submerse herself in Welsh for the rest of the summer and he would only speak to her in Welsh, which made some of the board games entertaining since not all of them translated that well. It was certainly challenging her vocabulary!

David held the door to the office open for her and Sophie made her way through. The others were already there and they exchanged greetings, swapping back to English since the Taylors didn't speak Welsh.

'Morning!' David said with a smile.

'Well, there's a sight I thought I might never see again!' Gwen said with a broad smile.

'Leave off, Mam,' David said, but there was no annoyance in his voice.

'Good to have the old David back, son,' Jeff said, and he reached up and squeezed his arm. Sophie could see in

Jeff's face the concern he had felt.

'Clearly Sophie's good spirits have rubbed off on you. I knew they would,' Gwen said sagely, and now Sophie felt herself blush. It wasn't like she had done much for David, except strong-arm him into teaching her Welsh in the evenings.

'You've worked wonders, love. Nothing his Dad or I have tried has helped a jot, but one week after you arrive, he's like a new person. No more moping and feeling sorry for himself.'

Sophie smiled through her embarrassment, but was a little surprised that they would so openly talk about a subject that was clearly so painful to David. She understood their relief that he was more like his old self, but it seemed a little off to Sophie. One glance at David told her that he felt the same. There was that all-too-familiar sag to his shoulders, and she felt like he was pulling back into himself. It was clear to Sophie that he needed rescuing, and fast. So she did what she had always done at awkward moments . . .

'So, you decided to keep the name? Of the caravan park?' Sophie said out loud, and the sudden change of subject seemed to pull everyone up short a bit. For a moment, everyone seemed to be staring and Sophie felt more embarrassed than she had earlier. But at least all eyes were on her now rather than David.

'My mum used to do some of the bookings for my grandparents and always used to complain that customers could never spell it, let alone say it,' Sophie said, her words coming out in a bit of a rush.

'It seemed to be part of the history of the place, pet. We didn't think we should mess with it, and besides, the locals were already suspicious of me since I'm not Welsh. Didn't want to do anything that might upset them more.' Jeff grinned at her, and Sophie wondered if he understood why she had changed the subject. She smiled gratefully back at him, and listened as he told the story of how he and Gwen had come to buy the site from her grandparents.

Sophie had just finished noting down in her book what her jobs were for the week — she did like to have a clear plan — when David interrupted her.

'You're down for the rubbish run, do you want a hand?'

Sophie blinked in surprise. David had been very vocal about how much he hated driving the trailer around the park and emptying the bins. It was right up there with cleaning the loos.

'You don't have to. I can manage,' she said, pushing her chair away from the table and standing up.

'I know I don't have to, but I want to.'

When Sophie looked at him he seemed a little ill at ease.

'Just wanted to say thanks for the rescue,' he said with a shrug, as if he wanted to downplay it.

Sophie studied him for a moment and wondered if now was the time to ask him what had happened.

'No problem, I get it. I mean, I'm not saying I understand what happened to you, but I know what it's like when everyone wants you to move on and you don't feel able to.'

David held the office door open for her and Sophie stepped through. She remembered how her mum had said sometimes the best way to get someone to open up is to not say anything, to give them space and let them feel the silence if they want to. So she led the way to the mini-tractor that they used to pull the trailer.

'I know they've been worried, and it's not like I've enjoyed seeing them like it, but they want me to be okay and . . . Well, it's not like I don't want to be okay, but I just don't know how.' David had a look of confusion on his face. 'Wow that really didn't make sense at all did it?'

'Actually, it did,' Sophie said with what she hoped was an encouraging smile. 'When Steve ended it the second time, I think everyone expected me to be angry, that I would yell and rage and then just move on.'

'You weren't angry?' David asked, as he fell into step with the tractor as it chugged forward.

'Sure, but that wasn't the overwhelming emotion.'

'Which was?' David asked, as he lifted a bulging black bin liner from the first set of bins and plonked it in the trailer. Sophie moved the tractor onwards to the next rubbish point.

'I don't know. Sad, embarrassed, lonely, heartbroken. Take your pick.'

David nodded and she knew that he was looking at her closely.

'I'm not sure that anyone can tell you how to feel or how long those feelings should last. It just is, and you have to work through it.'

Sophie focused on navigating around the small children that were playing with a ball in the road that ran through the caravans and tents.

'When Rebecca . . . ' David started to

speak, but the name seemed to catch in his throat.

'You don't have to tell me. I know how hard it is to talk about these things,' Sophie said.

David cleared his throat with an effort and Sophie saw the all-too-familiar flash of pain cross his face.

'When Rebecca was . . . gone . . . '

Sophie nodded; she knew it. She knew that David had suffered a personal tragedy — his girlfriend had died.

'It seemed like there was nothing left, like there was nothing of me left either.' David's voice seemed to break on the last word and Sophie slowed the tractor to a stop and reached out and squeezed his arm.

'It was like I didn't know what I wanted anymore. No, it was more than that. I didn't actually want anything anymore. So I left my job and came here. Everyone thought I was crazy, all my friends, even Mum and Dad didn't seem to get it.'

David stood by the tractor and since Sophie didn't want to stop him from sharing what he clearly needed to, she pulled on her gloves and started to lift the full bin bags into the trailer.

'When I teased you about coming to the back of beyond, it was only because I knew I had done it too. I walked away from a great job, my friends, my life, because of Rebecca. I just couldn't be there without her. Everything reminded me of her.'

David's eyes drifted across the site to all the families and couples who were preparing for their days.

'Believe me, I get it,' Sophie said. 'You need time. It's taken me three years,' she added, and found she was holding her breath. She had never said out loud the real reason that her dreams had been on hold for so long. She had come up with a whole range of excuses that she had shared with everyone else in her life, but right now she couldn't help but feel it was important for her to share this with

David. Especially since he had shared something so personal with her.

'That's a bit different. Aiden was sick. You were supporting your family through a terrible time. I've just been indulging myself.'

'Our situations weren't the same. Your loss was more significant than mine. And besides Aiden's illness really only lasted eighteen months. The rest of the time was all about Steve.'

Sophie had to look away, as she couldn't bear to see what David would make of her words. When she made herself look back, he was still wearing a look of confusion.

'Huh,' David said, and smiled. 'Who would have thought that all the way out here I would finally find someone who understands.'

Sophie held his gaze but was the first to look away, fearing that if she looked into his chocolate eyes for any longer she would lose her heart again. Lose it to someone who wasn't ready to love again, and maybe never would be.

9

'I have a surprise for you,' David said as he pulled the door to the van closed behind him.

'If it's a tin of tuna, you've got the wrong person,' Sophie said, closing the oven on the chicken casserole that was reheating.

'Are you suggesting that the only person I surprise around here is your cat?' he asked, with mock indignation.

Sophie raised an eyebrow. Not a day had gone by since she met David that he didn't bring some sort of gift for Maple. Sometimes it was food, sometimes it was a shop-bought toy, but recently he had taken to building her the ultimate cat scratching and sleeping tower. As far as Sophie was concerned, it just used up precious space in the van, but even she had to admit that Maple seemed very taken with the contraption. It was surprisingly endearing that David treated Maple like a person, since Sophie had always felt that way about her — although a tiny part of her, ridiculous as it may be, was also a little jealous.

'This is definitely for you. I doubt that Maple would be interested unless you leave it lying around and then I suspect she would ensure that it was filed carefully on the floor.'

Sophie looked up from making them both a cup of tea to see David placing a brown envelope on the small table that she had already set up with her laptop and the various Teach Yourself Welsh books she had bought.

'What is it?'

'Open it,' David said whilst tapping his lap to try and encourage Maple to come and sit near him. Maple just flicked him a glance and continued to studiously wash her paw, sat in what David had claimed was a throne at the top of the cat scratching tower. Sophie carried over the two cups of tea and put one in front of David. He took a sip and watched her open the envelope. Inside was a stack of paper, all written in Welsh. On closer inspection, Sophie could see that they were exam papers.

'Where did you get GCSE exam papers from?' Sophie asked, looking at him closely.

'Relax, they're mock papers, you're not cheating or anything.'

'Sorry, I just meant who did you get them from?'

David shrugged as if it was nothing.

'I asked an old school friend who's a teacher to see if they could get hold of any for you. They're a few years old, but I thought they would be good practice.'

Sophie started to flick through them and her heart sank a little. She was having trouble enough reading the questions, let alone formulating an answer.

'Relax Soph,' David said, reaching out an arm for her hand which had started to shake. 'You don't need to be able to do them now. We have plenty of time to get you up to scratch. This is just so you know what you are aiming for.'

Sophie let out her breath in a sigh. It seemed such an impossible task in the available time.

'Maybe I should have kept hold of them,' David said with a frown. 'They were supposed to be encouraging.'

Sophie forced herself to calm down.

'They're great, really, they are. And it's so kind of you. I just have to try not to think about the tests in week one too much. I get a little freaked out.'

'No freaking out, Ms Carson. We have plenty of time and you're making real progress. I reckon you could easily keep pace with your average reception class.' David was unable to keep a straight face and he let out a snort of laughter. Sophie rolled her eyes and thumped him on the arm.

'Not funny.'

'You should see your face!' David said as he tried to stop laughing. 'Seriously, you're doing just fine. I'll get you there, I promise.'

His voice was serious now, and Sophie felt comforted by it. She knew that he meant every word. She just hoped that she could live up to the challenge.

They had worked for an hour and Sophie felt a little more confident. David had tested her on some basic grammar and she had got all but one question right. Sophie placed a plate of casserole in front of David and then one in front of herself. Maple had been distracted by a few pieces of leftover chicken.

'So how are you doing?' Sophie asked.

'Okay, I guess. It's weird really, everyone else in my life made it quite clear that they thought talking about Rebecca wasn't helping and so they avoided the subject. If I brought her up they would quickly change the subject. Now I know that I can talk to you about her I feel less like talking about her.' He paused for a moment. 'Not sure if that's a good thing or a bad thing.'

Sophie swallowed her mouthful.

'What was she like?'

David gazed out of the window and Sophie wondered if she had killed the light-hearted mood. It was good to know that he felt he could talk to her about Rebecca but the fact that he never did was troubling, although she didn't know why.

'Smart,' he said, as if he were speaking to someone outside of the window. 'She's really smart. Way smarter than me.'

A small voice inside Sophie's head said, 'Clearly much smarter than you, then.' She tried to ignore the voice, which sounded just like Julie Trubeck, who had picked on her all through senior school.

'Successful, funny, popular, outgoing.'

The voice was back. 'You've got no chance.' Sophie forced herself to focus on what David was saying instead, since he was still talking.

'I miss her,' he said finally, turning his attention back to Sophie, who was quite glad he hadn't noticed her being so distracted by an imaginary voice in her head that she had heard little of his description of the love of his life.

'Of course you do,' Sophie said. 'I know it's not the same but I still miss Steve. I know, I know,' she said, holding up her hands as if to fend him off, even though David hadn't said anything. 'I shouldn't, but I do. The problem with other people is they only remember the bad stuff, the things that person did to hurt you, but I remember all the other things about Steve and that's what I miss.'

Now it was Sophie's turn to sigh at the memories. She made herself focus on her dinner and scooped up a mouthful of carrots.

'I don't think we're so different,' David said. 'We've both lost someone important to us that we loved. You are the first person that seems to really understand how I feel.' He said the words softly and Sophie felt her heart thump in her chest.

'I'm sure your mum and dad understand, David. They're lovely people,' Sophie said, feeling like the conversation might be veering into dangerous territory.

'They do, but not like you.'

David had finished eating and was leaning back against the sofa. He reached out a hand and gently pulled Sophie so that she found herself lying in the crook of his arm.

'Thank you,' he whispered, and she felt herself relax into him.

'For what?' she asked, although she wasn't sure she was ready to hear the answer. She wanted to be David's friend — okay, the truth was she wanted to be more than that. But she couldn't be the rebound girl, not again and not when David was clearly still recovering from the death of Rebecca. Who was perfect, said that little voice.

'For being you,' David said, resting

his chin on the top of her head. 'For being a kind and warm person. For . . . '

David's words were cut off by Maple, who had decided in that moment to leap from the heights of her throne onto David's lap.

'And of course for bringing this other fabulous person in to my life,' he said, as he stroked Maple's ears. 'Who knew I would turn out to be a cat person?'

'Maple wins even the most ardent anti-cat person over if she wants to,' Sophie said, not sure whether she was glad of her cat's interruption or if she wished that she had waited a few more moments so that David could have finished what he was going to say.

Maple started to meow, usually a sign she was ready for bed, which in her world meant everyone else should be too.

'You should probably go, it must be late,' Sophie said, wondering if her cat was actually right and that now would be a good time for the conversation to end.

'Do I have to?' David murmured into her hair, and she could feel her resolve weaken a little. Then the sensible part of her kicked in. David had lost his girlfriend. Two weeks ago he had been in the depths of despair, and while it was great that he was doing better now, he was by no means ready for a new relationship. Sophie had also experienced being the rebound girl, and there was no way she was going to put herself through that again.

Actually it was more important than that. David was special. She had known that almost as soon as she had met him — once he was a little less antagonistic, although perhaps even then she had seen something in him that made her want to help him. Sophie wondered as she lay in his arms, feeling as if she was finally home, if he could be the one. If she thought that was in any way a possibility, there was no way she would risk taking things too fast. What David needed was time and friendship, and since Sophie believed that the best relationships were built on a foundation of friendship before romance, that was what she was going to do.

She wriggled to free her arm so that she could see her watch.

'It's nearly midnight.' she said, and forced herself to sit up and gently lift away his arm. It was the last thing she wanted to do. She felt she could stay in his arms forever but she knew what she needed to do and she knew that it would be worth it.

'You need to go get some sleep. We have to get up early. We're on toilet duty, remember?'

David groaned and reached out for her arm as she tried to move away.

'You can't send me away to spend all night thinking about the terrible task that faces us tomorrow.'

'I won't,' Sophie said with a smile. 'I'm making you go home so you can get some sleep and be ready for tomorrow.' Sophie laughed as his face dropped.

'Can I at least take Maple with me?' he said in a voice that made him sound like a six-year-old begging for a chocolate treat.

Sophie raised an eyebrow.

'I know what you're doing. I've met your type before. All the treats, all the building grand cat-scratching posts. Are you trying to buy my cat's favour?'

Sophie stood with hands on her hips and tried to keep the grin off my face.

'Absolutely,' David said, smiling. 'Is it working?'

He addressed the last comment to Maple, who purred loudly as he tickled her ears and rolled onto her back so he could stroke her belly.

'Apparently!' Sophie said. 'Just remember, she's my cat. You can have visiting rights of course, but she lives with me.'

Sophie looked at Maple, who was starting to drool.

'Come on you,' she said, lifting

Maple off David's lap. He stood up and stretched, just like Maple. The cat reached out a paw for David's leg. Sophie gave her the look, which of course Maple ignored. Sophie opened the door to the bedroom and Maple pricked up her ears before trotting across the van. David and Sophie watched as Maple leapt up onto the bed, circled several times and then curled up in a ball.

'Goodnight, Maple,' David said. 'Goodnight, Soph.'

He leant in. Sophie held her breath, thinking he was going to kiss her. She wasn't sure that she would be able to resist kissing him back if he did. At the last minute, he kissed her gently on her cheek. He looked her full in the eyes, smiled and then left. Sophie put her hand to her chest. Her heart seemed to be going ten to the dozen. She shook herself and tried to remember what she had decided. Give it time, they needed time.

'We'll see you in the morning.'

10

Well, there was one thing to say about cleaning toilets, it was not in any way romantic. Sophie had dreamed of David all night, her mind running wild with how wonderful it would be if they were together, what a future they could have. She had woken in the morning feeling worn out and with her resolve weakened a little. Thank goodness for toilets! And she never thought she would have said that.

For David's part, he seemed to have slept well. He looked refreshed and more handsome than ever. His hair was a little long now, but it suited him somehow. There was real warmth in his eyes when he looked at her, which he did often.

'Finished?'

His voice cut through her imagination, which was once again off in a fantasy world of its own.

'Er, yeah,' Sophie said, hoping that David couldn't read her mind.

'Lunch?' he asked, clearly amused by how distracted she was.

'Sounds good. I'll go and get something sorted. I have some bread and ham I think,' Sophie said, brushing a strand of hair away from her forehead with the back of her hand.

'No,' David said, and Sophie turned to look at him. He looked amused.

'If you don't want bread and ham you may have to visit a supermarket.'

'No, not that either. I thought we could go out and eat?'

Sophie frowned. 'We have lots to do this afternoon,' she replied, while thinking to herself that a romantic lunch for two was not what she needed right now, if she was to stick to her plan.

'I spoke to Mum. She said we'd been working too hard and she's given us the afternoon off.'

'Really?' Sophie said, trying to work out what she should do next.

'You don't have to, if you don't want to. I just figured that we had been working pretty hard and you haven't seen much of the world outside this campsite.' David's face had dropped and Sophie knew that he was a little confused and maybe even hurt, which was not part of the plan.

'No, no. I'd love to. As long as your mum can cope? I mean I'd hate to leave all the jobs to her.'

David seemed placated, clearly assuming that Sophie's reluctance was related to her work ethic rather than any qualms about spending time with him. He slung an arm around her shoulders and Sophie winced at how comfortable she felt being so close to him. Thankfully David didn't seem to notice.

'Relax, Mum has it all sorted. And besides I think she's just happy that I'm doing better.'

Sophie smiled, she couldn't help it. Gwen wasn't the only one who felt like that.

'And since we all know that it is entirely down to you . . . ' He paused and pulled her in a little closer. 'And not forgetting our Maple. It's only right that I take you out and show you the sights.'

Sophie relaxed a little. David was right, they had been working hard. If you had asked her two weeks ago whether David would be taking her out for lunch she would have laughed. A lot. So what could it hurt? They would go out, as friends, and have a break from all the work.

Sophie was beginning to wonder if David was taking her to a pub in England. They had been in the car for what felt like hours, not that she minded. She wouldn't admit it to anyone, but she loved spending time with David, even if it was in a car navigating small Welsh lanes.

'Not far now,' David said. 'And it will be worth it, I promise. This place is a real find.'

He sounded almost anxious, so much

so that Sophie felt she should reassure him.

'I know it will. Now stop worrying and keep your eyes on the road,' she said as he turned to look at her for what felt like the hundredth time. She was beginning to enjoy the way he looked at her, but she also wanted to reach their destination in one piece.

'I'm glad you decided to come. You had me worried for a bit.'

Sophie turned to look out the window, aiming for casual and really hoping to avoid giving anything away on her face.

'I just don't want to take the mickey with your mum and dad. This job has been an absolute life saver. I couldn't have accepted my training place without it, and it was all so last minute.'

'Trust me, you are one of the hardest workers they have ever had, and you know my mum, she has her standards. They were more than happy for us to take an afternoon off, but it was on one condition.'

Sophie turned to look at him now, curious as to what that could be.

'You have to promise to relax and enjoy yourself. Mum's orders.'

Sophie laughed now and David joined her.

'I am relaxed, and I promise I will tell her that I've had a wonderful time, whatever happens. Happy?' she giggled.

'Very. And here we are,' he announced, just as if he had planned their arrival time to perfection.

The car had rounded a bend in the road and Sophie was treated to the most amazing views of the sea. For a moment she had no words. It really was a breath-taking view. They pulled into a small area of flattened grass on top of the cliff and got out. Sophie felt like she could see to the end of the world; the sea seemed to go on for ever. Although there was a stiff breeze, the sun was shining and reflecting off the sea as the waves rolled onto the sandy beach below. It was the Anglesey she remembered from her childhood, even though she knew she had never been here before.

She was aware that David was standing waiting for her but she couldn't quite draw her eyes away. When she finally did, he was smiling, a little triumphantly.

'I knew you'd like it.'

He held out his hand for her, and after a moment's pause she took it and allowed herself to be walked towards the edge of the cliff where a set of worn stone steps had been cut in. They wound their way down and found themselves on the beach. The beach, like the sea, seemed to go on forever. It was deserted except for two tiny dots in the distance, which Sophie was sure was a dog walker and their dog.

'It's amazing,' Sophie said, 'but I don't see anywhere to eat. Unless you have a picnic under your coat.'

'Have faith, Soph. We have to walk a little way, but it'll be worth it.'

They walked along the beach, hand in hand. The sensible part of Sophie's brain told her that she should gently take her hand away. This was precisely the wrong sort of message to send to David. But she couldn't quite bring herself to. Her hand seemed to fit into his perfectly, and besides, in the wind it was cold and his hand was toasty, she told herself. David seemed quite content to hold her hand and so she pushed down the nagging voice and let herself enjoy the sensation. They walked along, pointing out the occasional sight, but otherwise they were silent. It was the good, comfortable kind and Sophie felt like they had known each other for years rather than weeks.

Tucked under the cliff edge they came to a small café. The weather-worn sign, 'Pirate's Rest', swung in the breeze. Sophie could see that the back half of the café was swallowed by the cliff and she realised that it must be part of a cave. The front half of the café was all windows and so allowed its patrons to enjoy not only the food but the view as well.

'It can get pretty busy, so I asked Hywel to reserve us a table in the window.'

David stepped across the patio area that would hold tables and chairs in finer weather and opened the door. Sophie stepped through and was hit by a wavy of cosy warmth, from the log burner in the middle of the café and the noise of people enjoying themselves. Nearly every table was full; people were eating and drinking and dogs sat patiently waiting to go back out for a walk. There was one table free in the window, just as David had promised, and he led her to it. Sophie didn't know where to look first, the inside of the café, which was full of people and knick-knacks, or the amazing view of the beach and the sea beyond.

'I take it from the open-mouthed expression that you like it?' David asked, with an air of innocence. Sophie looked at him.

'Are you kidding? This is amazing! How can you not like Anglesey when you know of a place like this?' She had said it before she had time to think about the last comment but David smiled.

'I think you can have your favourite place somewhere but not love the entire island.'

Sophie considered this. She could see why this was David's favourite place. She was certain if she stayed here much longer it would become hers. A woman bustled over and greeted David in Welsh, asking if the table was to his liking and telling him off for leaving it so long between visits. David laughed.

'I've been busy working. You know what a slave driver my mum can be.'

The woman, whose name was Bethan, cuffed him lightly across the shoulder.

'I shall tell your mother you said that. How's Jeff's leg?'

'Another few weeks in plaster and then some intensive physio. They're hopeful he'll be back to his usual self by the end of the summer.'

Bethan turned to Sophie now and gave her a warm smile, which Sophie returned.

'And you must be Sophie. I've heard a lot about you.'

Sophie raised her eyebrows in surprise.

'Gwen tells me you have been a real help at the campsite and that you've managed to jolly David out of his foul mood.'

Sophie laughed. She had always known that this part of Wales was close-knit, but it seemed that everyone really did know everyone else's business. Some people might be worried about this, but it was one of the many things that Sophie loved about the place.

'Now, what can I get you both?'

They ordered their food and then turned to gaze out of the window. Bethan soon returned with their order and they tucked in. It was proper homemade food and so they concentrated on eating without talking, beyond the odd comment.

When David had finished he cleared his throat and Sophie had a sudden sense of dread. Her sensible side had been right. She had given David the wrong impression — well, maybe not the wrong impression; more like the wrong impression for right now. What David needed was time, time to heal and recover, time to work out what, and more importantly, who, he wanted in his life. She knew that if they rushed into a relationship now it would only end badly and she had been the rebound girl before. The pain of that memory made her sit up and ready herself for the gentle rebuff that she had rehearsed.

'I wanted to talk to you, actually,' David said, seeming suddenly nervous.

'Oh?' Sophie said, with a question-ing eyebrow. 'Is it that I am the slowest learner of Welsh you have ever met?' she added, hoping to lighten the mood. She failed, as David frowned just a little.

'No, you're doing fine. I keep telling you that.'

He sounded a little exasperated; Sophie was reminded of the David she had first met, and her heart sank. Something told her that he was not going to take well what she needed to say, even if it was for both their sakes. She watched as he took a deep breath and blew it out.

'It's about you and me, Soph. The thing is, I like you.'

'I like you too,' Sophie said, feeling like she needed to tell him that before she had to tell him no.

'I mean, *really* like you.'

Even though Sophie knew it was coming, it was like a blow to the stomach. She felt all the air go out of her lungs. They were the words that she longed to hear, but she knew that they had to wait. They had to give him time. She opened her mouth to speak, scared that if she didn't speak now she would chicken out and head down the road which would end in doomed romance, but David held up his hand.

'I know what you're thinking. When you arrived I was, quite frankly, depressed. You helped change that.'

Sophie's heart clenched.

'Before you get too worried, I know I have a long way to go. I feel better than I have in months, but I spent so long feeling sorry for myself that I don't think I've really got to grips with what happened.'

Sophie was starting to feel confused. She was no longer sure she had any idea where this was going.

'So I know that I need time.'

The words were like magic to Sophie's ears.

'I think you do, too,' she said quietly.

David nodded vigorously. 'I need to get my head straight, but the thing is I don't want to lose you in the meantime.'

'Lose me?' Sophie said, with the ghost of a smile on her lips.

'I know I'm asking a lot . . . ' David's voice drifted off and he looked out the window lost in thought.

'I'm not really sure what you are asking me.'

Sophie almost couldn't breathe. Could it be possible that they were both on the same page; that they were so in tune they had come to the same conclusion about their relationship?

David cleared his throat. 'What I'm asking, Soph, is if you will wait for me. I know I'm asking a lot, but the thing is, I really like you. Actually, I think it's more than just like.'

Sophie's heart jumped as he ran his hand through his hair.

'And it's because of that that I know I need time.'

He looked at her now and she could see agony on his face. She reached out and placed her hand over his and smiled.

'I really like you, too. And I think it's more than just like.'

He looked into her eyes and his expression held such hope that she thought she might cry.

'And I think you are right, I think you need time. I suspect we both do.' Sophie blew out a breath and laughed. 'I was worried that you were going to want to rush in, but I've had that experience before and, as you know, it didn't end well.'

Now David squeezed her hand and she knew that he understood how bad that had been for her.

'So, we stay friends for now,' he said, and Sophie nodded, 'but we don't date anyone else for a bit until we have got ourselves sorted and we can work out what we want to do next.'

Sophie nodded again and smiled. She couldn't believe this was happening, and happening in the way it was supposed to.

'You're sure?' David said, looking momentarily worried. 'I don't want to put you in an awkward position, or be all possessive or whatever.'

He rustled his hair again. Sophie raised a hand to his cheek and made him look at her.

'I'm one hundred percent sure, David. I know how I feel about you and I can wait until you are ready. I want to.'

David lifted Sophie's hand to his lips and kissed it gently.

'You have no idea how worried I've been! I was sure that I was reading you wrong, or that you wouldn't want to wait.'

Sophie laughed; he had no idea how similar they really were.

11

Sophie was beginning to think that fairy tales and dreams really did come true and that sometimes life did work out.

It had been over a month since the conversation at the Pirate's Rest and life had been near perfect. Sophie and David worked together all day and then spent most evenings together, learning Welsh (Sophie), learning the rules of board games (David) and being spoilt rotten (Maple). If Sophie was writing a book on how to ensure your romance lasts for good, she was sure that she had found the answer. They were good friends now, she knew a lot about David and he knew a lot about her. Sophie would go as far as to say that they had no secrets. David talked more about what had happened, and although he was sometimes quiet and withdrawn, Sophie was sure that he was moving forwards and that one day they would be able to move on from 'just being friends'. Although, if she was being really honest with herself, she knew that her heart already had. She loved David, she was sure of it now, and she was also certain that her future lay with him.

David's approach to their jobs on the caravan site had also changed. Where at first they had worked in silence and he seemed to take any opportunity to be as far away from her possible, now he pretty much insisted that they did all of the jobs together, even if it took longer.

Sophie had just dumped the last black bin liner in the large metal bins near the site office when a slick, black, jeep-like car pulled up in front of the office. Not the usual vehicle for caravaners and campers, but as Sophie had learnt in her time at the site, it took all sorts. She pulled off the gardening gloves that she used when doing bin collection and pushed her fringe off her forehead. The weather was warm and garbage duty was hard work.

'I wonder who that is?' Sophie said out loud to David, who was round the back of the bins unhitching the trailer from the small tractor. She waited for him to reply, but although he had walked around the bin to stand beside her, he stood in silence. She looked at him curiously — since David had found his voice, he rarely stopped talking — but was then distracted by a tall woman, a few years older than her and much better dressed, who stepped out of the car. She looked around and then her eyes settled on David and she lifted her hand to wave, before dropping it uncertainly. David's face seemed to close up, just as it had when Sophie had first met him. Sophie wanted to ask him who this woman was, but his face and her experience told her it was better not to ask. Without even looking at her, David strode across the gap between them and started to talk in quiet but harsh tones to the woman.

Sophie felt it was wrong to stare but

somehow couldn't help herself. Who was this woman and why was David so upset? The bell on the office door jingled and Gwen came out, closely followed by Jeff on his crutches.

'What's she doing here?' Gwen demanded, not bothering to keep her voice down.

Now Sophie was feeling bewildered. It was like watching a TV programme in a foreign language with no subtitles. She had no idea what was happening.

'Now Gwen, you need to let David handle this.'

Jeff looked across at Sophie and smiled, but there was no real happiness on his face. Instead, he looked worried.

Sophie couldn't bear it any longer, she had to know what was happening and since David didn't appear to want to tell her she knew what she had to do.

'Gwen,' she said, walking over to the pair, 'who is that?'

Gwen turned to look at her as if she'd only just realised that Sophie was there. Her eyes glistened with anger.

'That's the girl who broke my boy's heart. That's Rebecca.'

Sophie felt as if all the air had been squeezed out of her lungs. Black dots started to dance in front of her eyes and she recognised the tell-tale signs. She was going to faint. But suddenly there was a more overwhelming emotion that forced air back into her lungs. She realised that underneath the shock was anger, real fiery anger. David had lied to her.

'But I thought Rebecca had died,' Sophie managed to force out. More than anything right now she needed to know the truth. She pushed down the shock, which was swiftly being followed by agony, and focused on the anger.

'Whatever gave you that idea?' Gwen said sharply, before seeing the look on her face. She moved quickly to put her arm around Sophie's shoulder. Sophie wanted to push her away, not sure that she could bear to be touched in that moment, but Gwen's face held over-whelming concern.

'Our David never told you she died, did he?'

Gwen was shocked now too, and Sophie knew that any minute it was going to turn into anger and it would be directed at David. Sophie's mind raced through every conversation she had ever had with David and then it hit her.

'No, he never did. I mean, he never told me exactly what happened.'

Sophie could feel the flames rise up her face. David had never said that Rebecca had died, he had simply talked about losing her. It was Sophie who had decided that Rebecca must have died. Sophie had decided that only the death of a partner could cause a person that level of despair. What else could cause a person to speak about that partner in tones of loss, with never a word of anger or reproachment?

'I . . . I just . . . ' Sophie wasn't sure she could say the words out loud. 'It's my fault,' she said finally. 'I just put two and two together and got five.'

'Oh pet, I assumed he had told you all about it. If I had known, I would have told you myself,' Gwen said kindly.

Sophie knew that she needed to get out of this situation. She needed to head back to her van, fall into bed and shut out the world.

'I have to go,' she said, unable to take her eyes off David and Rebecca who continued to trade words. Gwen opened her mouth to speak, but a warning look from Jeff left the words unspoken.

''Course you do, Sophie. You head off and make yourself a cup of tea. Let us know if you need anything.'

He smiled so kindly that Sophie thought she would start crying there and then, but she swallowed back the tears. There would be plenty of time for tears later. She wasn't going to stand in the middle of the campsite with David and his girlfriend looking on. As the word 'girlfriend' popped into her head, she knew it would be the final straw that would break down the wall of tears, so she murmured a thank you and then turned and walked away. She wanted to run but forced her fingernails into the palm of her hand to hold back the emotion and made herself walk at a pace which suggested she was unbothered by the events that had just unfolded in front of her.

★　★　★

Sophie ignored the knocking on the door and waited for the person to try the door handle again. She always left it unlocked when she was in so that David could come and go as he pleased, but today she had purposely locked it. She didn't want to speak to him right now, she wasn't sure she ever wanted to speak to him again. She had spent all evening trying to wrestle her thoughts into some kind of order. There was anger at David, but also anger at herself. Embarrassment that she had jumped to her own conclusions, and then anger at David again, that he had never told her the whole story of what had happened. In the early hours, she had railed against him in her mind. She'd thought they had no secrets. She'd thought he had told her all there was to know about him and Rebecca, but he had left out one important point. Rebecca could walk back into his life at any moment, as she had the afternoon before.

She was angry with herself that she had never outright asked him. How could she have been so stupid? Why hadn't she asked Jeff or Gwen about it? They would have told her and then she could have saved herself some of this pain, which was all too familiar. She had once again put her heart out in the world and a man had trampled on it. After promising her everything. Once again, she wondered if she had read too much into his words, if she had made the story up that she wanted to hear. When he had said he needed time, maybe it was because he thought Rebecca might come back to him and that he didn't want to enter into a new relationship just in case.

She pulled the pillow over her head to drown out the insistent knocking and to try and smother her own thoughts. She felt a weight jump onto the bed; Maple started to pace, before mewing pitifully. Clearly, she was hungry. Sophie gave herself a shake. Just because her world felt like it was ending, there was no reason for Maple to suffer. She shuffled out of bed, opened the cupboard containing the cat food and fed Maple, who fell on her dish as if she hadn't been fed for weeks.

'Oh Maple, what are we going to do?' Sophie said aloud. Maple paused briefly to look up and the look said it all — 'Pick yourself up and get on with what you've got to do.'

'You're right. I need to go to work. Whatever David's done, I have a job to do. I'm paid to help Gwen and Jeff, and that's what I'm going to do.'

A voice at the door made her jump.

'I'll see you around, then.'

David's voice was dull and unhappy. She winced as she remembered quite how thin the walls of the van were, and the fact that if you weren't careful every word you said could be heard by someone standing outside the door.

A glance at the clock told her she had no time to shower. She used a baby wipe to freshen her face, scraped a comb through her hair before tugging it into a ponytail, and pulled on her campsite uniform. The mirror told her she looked tired and worn, but it was the best she could do. She was going to hold her head high. There would be no public moping. She would get on with her work cheerfully and efficiently, as she had always done. When she was finished, she could return to the comfort of her van and wallow in private.

A quick glance out of the window in the lounge area of the van told her that David was gone. She opened the window so that Maple could come and go as she pleased, told her to behave herself, and then cautiously opened the door. She knew what jobs were allocated to her today and that meant she could just get on with them, and avoid having to go to the office. Avoiding talking to people seemed to be the way to go.

Sophie felt in her pocket for the keys to the storage unit, opened it, and pulled out the trolley that contained the cleaning stuff for the vans. She helped herself to a pile of fresh bedding and a laundry bag and then trundled the trolley to the first van that had been vacated the day before, which would need to be made ready for its next visitors, arriving that evening. She tried for a casual air but she knew she was scanning the area for any sign of David.

She unlocked the van door and started to cart the supplies she would need into the van before closing the door firmly behind her. She let herself have a moment of relief that he had decided to stay away.

Sophie opened the door to the

bedroom that held the bunk beds and started to pull the used bedding off each mattress. She remade the beds, dusted and hoovered, and then headed to the main bedroom which housed a double bed. She opened the door and then jumped in fright. David was sat on the bed with his head in his hands.

She fought down a squeal of fright and aimed for quiet indignation.

'What are you doing here?' she said, working hard to keep her voice steady.

'I needed to talk to you and you wouldn't open the door.'

Sophie waited a moment and forced herself to compose a reply.

'That's because I don't want to talk to you right now.'

'Please Soph,' he said, looking up. 'I need to explain.'

'Maybe you need to think about what I need right now,' Sophie said, and knowing that she was losing any chance of remaining in control, she turned and ran down the van steps and away from David.

12

It was happening exactly the way she had hoped it wouldn't. Sophie was running across the campsite heading for the safety of her van with tears running down her face. She had tried to hold them back with no luck. She was red-faced and her breath came out in heaves, not just from the effort of running but because of the sobs that she could no longer hold back. As she ran, she could hear David calling out her name and the sound of his footsteps as he ran after her. She tried to block out all the faces that appeared outside caravans and tents as she ran past. Most curious, some sympathetic. She suspected that the drama that had unfolded outside the site office yesterday had done the gossip rounds. She heard another voice calling her name, a woman's voice with a Welsh accent. She knew it was Gwen's but could do nothing more than hold up a hand to indicate that she couldn't talk now, and keep running.

She yanked open the door of her van with such force that she made Maple jump in the middle of her morning washing routine. She slammed the door behind her and turned the latch so that she would not have any unwelcome visitors. Sophie felt her knees collapse beneath her and she gave into it and sat down on the floor. Maple, picking up on her distress, didn't return to her washing but instead padded over and rubbed her head against Sophie's hands.

'Oh Maple,' she said softly, as Maple lifted her head to kiss her check. 'What am I going to do?'

She leaned her head against the wall and let her knees drop so that Maple could settle in her lap. Sophie stroked her and listened to her purr, not knowing what else to do. Maple's ears pricked up at the sound of voices that drifted through the open window.

'Leave her be, David. I think you've done enough!'

It was Gwen's voice, indignant and angry at her son.

'Mum, please, you don't understand. I need to talk to Sophie. I need to explain.'

'You need to think about her, not yourself. Go get on with your jobs and let her alone.'

'I have to check that she's okay first.' David's voice was determined.

'Do you think she wants that right now? Go get on, and while you're at it you can get Sophie's jobs done as well. She's not going to be in a fit state do anything much today.'

There was silence and Sophie suspected a battle of wills was going on.

'Go,' Gwen said, more gently this time. 'I'll check up on Sophie, and yes I will let you know how she is, although I think we can all guess. Best thing you can do is get her jobs done so she doesn't need to worry. Go!'

Sophie waited, holding her breath and trying to decide whether she was going to open the door when the inevitable knock came. She really didn't want to, not because it was Gwen but just because she didn't want to talk to anyone. However, the good manners that had been drilled into her as a child told her that it was rude to just simply ignore Gwen. When the knock came, it was gentle.

'Sophie, love? It's only Gwen. Can I come in?'

Maple stood up and stepped off Sophie's lap. Sophie allowed herself a sigh, but she unlocked the door and opened it so that Gwen could step inside.

'Ah, Sophie, you've done wonders with the place.'

Sophie looked around at all the things she had done to make the place feel more like her home. She had made new curtains and several throw pillows, as well as putting up photos of her family.

'Can I sit down?' Gwen asked.

Sophie, remembering her manners, said, 'Of course, Gwen. I'm sorry, I'm a bit all over the place today.'

Sophie thought to herself that didn't really cover it.

'I know you are, Anywylyd. And I'm not surprised. Come and sit down with me.'

Gwen patted the seat beside her and, not knowing what else to do, Sophie sat down.

'Rebecca's coming must have been more of a shock to you than it was to me, and I was pretty shocked.'

Sophie managed a small smile but couldn't find any words to say.

'If I'd have known what you thought, if I had known what impression David had given you . . . Well, I'd have given him a clip round the ear and set you straight.' Gwen reached out for one of Sophie's hands and squeezed.

'With you both getting on so well, I told myself not to interfere. It never occurred to me that David hadn't told you. I don't suppose I will be listening to my own advice again any time soon,' she finished, and Sophie had to squeeze her hand back. Gwen and Jeff had been so good to her, and none of this was their fault, whatever Gwen might think.

'It's no one's fault, Gwen, probably not even David's.'

Gwen's eyes flashed and Sophie knew that Gwen wasn't ready to agree on that point yet.

'I mean it. It's not like he told me that Rebecca had died. I just assumed from what he said and the way he was.'

Gwen snorted. 'He always was a bit of a drama queen. Had his heart broken by a young lass in secondary school, you'd have thought he had been orphaned the way he was carrying on. Don't get me wrong, no mother wants to see their child in pain, but David has trouble moving on. That is until you came.'

'I'm glad I could help,' Sophie said, and then surprised herself by bursting into tears. Crying on her sort-of-boyfriend's mother had not been her intention.

Gwen gathered Sophie up in her arms and for a moment Sophie felt like she was back at home with her own mum. Gwen rubbed her back and let her cry. When Sophie thought she had cried enough, at least for now, she moved so that she was sat by herself again.

'I'm sorry. I don't want to put you in the middle of this.'

'You're not. David's done that all by himself. I never liked Rebecca and that was before she broke his heart.'

Sophie winced. Although in some ways it was good to hear, she couldn't help but feel guilty. Rebecca could hardly be blamed for being alive, and as for breaking David's heart, she had no idea what had actually happened, since David had never told her.

'Maybe it's just all a misunderstanding,' Sophie said with a sniff. 'Perhaps I should talk to David. Jumping to conclusions is what got me into this mess. Maybe I should actually ask him outright what's going on.'

Gwen smoothed down Sophie's hair.

'I think you should talk to him, if you want to, but when you're ready.'

Sophie opened her mouth to speak, but Gwen held up a hand.

'Don't be speaking to him when you're not ready just because you're worried he's upset. It will do him good to stew for a bit.'

Sophie couldn't hide her surprise.

'I love that boy with all my heart, but sometimes I want to shake him,' she said, standing up. 'This might well be a lesson he needs to learn.'

Gwen moved to the door.

'Do you need anything? I can bring you over some dinner if you don't fancy cooking.'

'I'm fine Gwen, thank you. I'm feeling much better. I could get back to work.'

Gwen raised her eyebrows. 'I think not. Part of the lesson David needs to learn ought to be practical and getting him to do all your jobs seems like a good place to start. And besides, hard work never killed anyone.'

And with that Gwen was gone and Sophie was left again to try and wrestle her emotions into some sort of order. Not knowing what else to do, she decided to go to bed. She had hardly slept the night before and she was exhausted. She would work out what she wanted to say to David, and when she wanted to say it, after her nap.

★   ★   ★

Sophie stirred. She was lying on her side and Maple was curled in a ball against her chest. Sensing that Sophie was awake, Maple started to purr and Sophie stroked her ears.

'What should I do, Maple? Do you have any ideas after your nap?'

Maple looked serious and reached out a paw to tap Sophie on the nose. This, Sophie knew, was a clear signal that it was time for cat treats. Sophie stretched and looked at her watch. It was nearly Maple's tea time anyway. She got up, smoothed down her hair and headed towards the kitchen. As she dropped a few treats into Maple's bowl, she couldn't resist looking across to David's van. She could see the shadow of a figure moving around which meant that David had finished work and was home.

'David's home,' she said to Maple, who looked over with her ears pricked up. Maple headed to the open window and with a quick look over her shoulder disappeared out. Sophie was sure she knew where she was headed. David tended to keep all sorts of meaty treats for Maple, none of which were particularly good for her, but Maple wasn't at all worried about her health.

Sophie watched as Maple stalked around the van and up to the steps that David had left in place so that she could easily reach the window he left open, just in case she felt like a change of location for any of the many naps she took during the day. Maple disappeared from view and Sophie forced herself to turn away and focus on something else. Not knowing what else to do, she started to make a cup of tea. Crashing noises from next door made her drop everything, and she was out of her van before she had time to think about whether she was ready to speak to David. Something was happening next door and it didn't sound good.

She found herself at the top of the small set of steps that led to David's front door. A second crashing sound brought her up short. Either David was throwing things around or he was being burgled, and she didn't think she could ignore it either way. She tapped on the door but there was no response and so she pushed it open.

'David?' she called out.

She stopped in her tracks. The van had been tidied; more than that, it was orderly. Everything, it seemed, had found its spot. It looked nothing like

David's home anymore, even though it was still full of everything he owned. Sophie wondered briefly if David was one of those people who tidied when they were upset and then discounted it. If that were true, his place would have been immaculate when Sophie had first entered it to retrieve Maple.

'Can I help you?' a cool voice said, and Sophie jumped. It wasn't David's voice, and it was clearly not a burglar since they tended to make a mess rather than clear one up. Sophie spun on the spot and found herself face to face with Rebecca, who was holding a broom.

'Er . . . ' was all Sophie could think to say. Rebecca was studying her and Sophie was acutely aware that she had just woken up from a nap and hadn't washed her hair for a few days. Rebecca, naturally, looked perfect and was expensively dressed.

'I'm Sophie, Sophie Carson. I live in the van next door,' Sophie said, her manners kicking in. She held out a hand, but as Rebecca made no move to shake it, she dropped it to her side.

'Rebecca Bowerman. I'm a friend of David's,' Rebecca said, with an emphasis on the word friend that indicated she was much more.

'You cleaned up,' Sophie said, feeling the need to distract Rebecca from her detailed scrutiny of her.

'Well, I couldn't stay here with it the way it was. It looked like one of the homeless towns in the underpass near to where I work.' Rebecca's voice was without humour. 'He always has been untidy, but this was way worse.'

Rebecca looked around and her expression said that she felt the same about the campsite.

'I guess he was pretty upset when you and he broke up.'

Sophie couldn't quite believe she had said that out loud, but Rebecca's attitude was annoying her and also, she wondered if Rebecca would fill in some of the blanks that David had left.

'It was only ever temporary,' Rebecca said.

Now it was Sophie's turn to look unimpressed.

'He didn't seem to think so,' she said, crossing her arms.

'Well men, particularly David, can be so funny about things. One little disagreement and apparently it's all over. They pack up your things and move to the middle of nowhere to work on a campsite.' Rebecca now made no effort to hide her disdain of David's life choices and the place that Sophie loved.

Sophie opened her mouth to send back a retort when the door to the caravan opened.

'Hey Maple, what are you doing out here?' David's voice carried into the van and both Sophie and Rebecca remained silent. David's attention was on fussing Maple, so he didn't realise he had other visitors until he was practically standing next to Sophie. On any other day the look of shocked confusion on his face would have been funny, but Sophie was in no mood to laugh. In the last twenty-four hours, she had discovered that the man she thought she had fallen in love with was seemingly still hung up on his ex-girlfriend, she herself was a fool, and now this place, that she loved so much, had been mocked by the aforementioned ex.

Maple hissed and this seemed to bring everyone back to the present.

'What are you doing here?' he asked and Sophie wasn't sure whether he was referring to her or Rebecca.

'I heard banging noises and I thought you might be being burgled,' Sophie said, clenching her jaw to try and stop the blush that was trying to form. There was no way she was going to tell him that she had wanted to talk to him. 'And I thought Maple might be in here,' she added, a little weakly.

'Who's Marple?' Rebecca asked.

'Maple,' both Sophie and David corrected in unison.

David looked at her, but Sophie couldn't bear to see the possible rejection in his face and so looked away.

'Oh, the cat,' Rebecca said. 'I thought it was a stray so chased it out with the broom. I thought it might start peeing everywhere and I'd just cleaned up.'

Sophie glared at Rebecca and made up her mind. She was leaving and taking her cat with her. David, for his part, seemed to have just realised that his van looked nothing like it had that morning. He stared around as if he was a just-arrived visitor on an alien planet.

'You tidied up,' he said. It was more of a statement than a question.

Sophie moved down the van and sidled past him.

'Soph, don't go,' he said.

'I really think she should,' Rebecca said. 'You said you wanted to talk.'

Sophie scooped up Maple, who didn't seem all that keen on leaving despite the fact that Rebecca's nose wrinkled whenever she looked at her, and, head in the air, she opened the door and walked down the steps. She marched over to her own van and closed the door firmly behind her. Once inside, Maple seemed determined to re-enact the great escape, and so Sophie pulled the window to, to prevent her slipping out to David's again. Maple sat, looking plaintively out of the window, and occasionally tapping the window catch.

'You heard the lady,' Sophie said. 'David wants to speak with her.'

Sophie's mind raced. Now that Rebecca was back, they clearly had a lot to talk about. Like, when he would leave and move back to London. How he would get his old job back. Where they would live. Perhaps Rebecca had kept the flat on, and David would move back straight away.

Sophie clenched her fists. She was going to drive herself mad going on like this. What she needed was a distraction. Her gaze found the Welsh books on her small bookshelf and she knew what she needed to do. If David was leaving, she would need to work even harder to be ready for the exams at the start of the course. There was no way she was going to let another man get in the way of her dreams.

13

Sophie turned over in bed and sighed. She had silenced her alarm clock twice now, and if she didn't get up soon she was going to be late for the morning meeting.

It was Monday, and that meant the whole team got together for breakfast and to discuss the jobs that needed doing that week. The children had broken up for the summer the Friday before, which meant the site was heading for its busiest six weeks of the year. Sophie was normally up before her alarm, ready for the day ahead, but since Rebecca had arrived her world seemed to have tilted on its axis and everything felt like it was out of place. The sound of a cat scratching furniture somewhere in the van was the push that Sophie needed and she leapt out of bed.

'Okay, okay! I get the message,' she said, knowing she was grumbling at her cat, who was sat with a butter wouldn't melt face, as if she hadn't been destroying someone else's property just a few seconds before. Sophie opened the cat food cupboard to find that it was empty. Pulling open the other cupboard and the fridge door told her that there was nothing remotely resembling cat food in her van. Another thing that was out of character for her — she hadn't bothered to go shopping. This wasn't so much of a problem for her own needs, but unfortunately the little shop in the site office didn't sell cat food.

She glanced at her watch. She hadn't time to go to nearest shop, which was a good ten-minute drive. She pulled the curtains as Maple wound around her legs. The solution was staring her in the face. David always had food for Maple; not always cat food, but definitely something that she could eat. David's curtains were drawn and she could see a light was on, so he was clearly up.

Sophie sat down on the sofa and chewed a fingernail, another bad habit she had started since it had all happened. It had been two weeks and she had been civil to David, talking when it was necessary for work, but no more. The longer it went on, the harder it seemed to start the conversation about what this all meant for them. David, for his part, had taken his mother's advice and was leaving Sophie to herself.

Maple jumped up on to the sofa and started clawing at her pyjama bottoms. It was no good, Sophie really didn't have a choice. She would go next door and ask David for some cat food. They couldn't go on avoiding each other. Sophie felt like she was stuck in limbo and it was starting to drive her mad. She had to know. She had to know what was going on and what that meant for her and David, or if there even was a 'her and David' anymore. She had to start somewhere and maybe a tin of cat food could be the answer.

Sophie went to her bedroom and pulled on the tracksuit that she kept for walking over to the shower block, pushed her feet into her shoes and headed out the door before she could talk herself out of it. Maple was following her; clearly, she had picked up on the plan.

At the top of the three small steps to David's van, Sophie paused. If Maple hadn't been there, she knew she would have fled back to her own van. Holding her breath, she listened at the door. Aside from the sounds of someone moving around inside, she could hear nothing. Tentatively, she knocked on the door, which opened almost immediately.

'Sophie?' David said, sounding surprised. 'Are you okay?'

His face creased in a frown of concern and Sophie's heart skipped a beat as she was reminded how much she missed him. She tried a smile, but it felt out of practice, and she wasn't sure what message her face was giving.

'I've run out of cat food, haven't been to the shops for a few days. I wondered if you had any? I'll pay you back,' she added hurriedly.

'Don't be daft,' David said, and now it was his turn to try out a smile, which was a little awkward but, Sophie could see, was reflected in his eyes. 'I have a stash. I'll grab you a couple of tins and some treats so you don't need to worry about the shops straight away.'

Sophie thought that he was going to invite her in, but instead he simply turned and made his way into the kitchen area of the van. He returned with the promised tins and handed them over.

'I shut the window,' David said. 'I thought you might want Maple to stay away.'

He winced at what he had said and she could feel his eyes searching her expression for some signs of what she was feeling.

Sophie rearranged the cans in her

arms and then forced herself to look up.

'I guess we should find some time to talk at some point.' Once the words were out Sophie felt a sense of relief.

'I'd really like that,' David said. 'Maybe we could meet up after work tonight? We could go to the pub. You know, neutral territory, and all that.'

Sophie nodded. 'Sounds good,' she said, and she had to admit it did. She missed him; she missed her friend and confidant, and she missed the man she thought was the one.

'Okay then. I'd best go feed the starving critter.'

David rewarded the comment with a grin which seemed to freeze in place when a voice sounded from within the van.

'Who are you talking to? It's too early to get up, come back to bed.'

Sophie felt as if her world had been shaken by yet another earthquake. She now knew what he wanted to talk to her about. He was taking her out to a pub, to neutral territory as he put it, to tell her that he was back with Rebecca.

They stared at each other for a couple of heartbeats and David at least had the decency to look embarrassed.

'I'll see you later then?' he asked, lamely.

'I don't think we have much to talk about, do you?' Sophie said, and then turned on her heel and marched back to her own van, cursing herself for giving him another opportunity to hurt and embarrass her.

Sophie dressed quickly. She wanted to arrive at the meeting before David. That meant she could choose a seat as far away from him as possible and there would be no opportunity for him to try and 'explain'. She wasn't sure why she was so upset. The reality of the situation had been staring at her for two weeks. All that had happened this morning was confirmation of what she knew to be true.

Sophie felt a flash of anger. He could have told her though. He could have just come out and explained himself, but that didn't seem to be David's thing. He never explained things, not fully, which is what had led Sophie to this ridiculous situation in the first place. That, and her desire to help him. She had risked her heart again, to help someone who, at the time, didn't seem to want to help himself and where had it got her? The same old pain, the same old long nights of crying and no sleep. All that it had really done was risk her dream, again. She could have slapped herself for being such an idiot. But, she told herself firmly, what was done was done. She couldn't change it but what she could do was try to protect her future. Enough about David, she needed to concentrate on herself. She needed to concentrate on her Welsh.

Sophie was greeted by Jeff and a warm smile. A quick check of the small back room told her that her plan had worked. She had arrived before David.

'How are you doing, pet?' Jeff asked, sympathetically.

'I'm fine,' Sophie said firmly, her new

attitude in place.

Jeff looked unconvinced so she smiled at him.

'Really, Jeff, I'm fine. I'm happy for David. It's clearly what he wants.'

Jeff's look suggested he remained unconvinced, but at that moment Paul and Lydia bustled in with their normal cheerful greetings, so Sophie smiled and took a seat that would place her between Gwen and Paul. After breakfast, it was clear that David was a no-show and Sophie allowed herself a sense of relief. She needed a bit more time to get her new attitude firmly in place before she was ready to test it on him, and besides, she had something she wanted to ask Gwen. It would be easier if David wasn't around.

'I'll help with the washing up,' Sophie said, as the doorbell that warned of incoming visitors to the office sounded.

'I'll go greet the new people,' Jeff said, looking understanding.

Sophie sighed. Jeff clearly thought that she wanted to have a heart to heart with Gwen, which couldn't be further from the truth. She had expended far too much time and energy on the David situation and she didn't want to talk about it anymore. Not that there was much to talk about. No, what she needed to talk to Gwen about was a favour.

Sophie picked up the tea towel and started to dry up the glasses.

'Gwen, I have a bit of a favour to ask.'

'Anything, sweetheart, you know that.'

'Well,' Sophie said, picking up some cutlery, 'I've got really behind on my Welsh and was hoping that you could maybe help me out?'

Gwen laughed. 'Of course, pet. Although I've heard you speak and you sound just fine to me.'

'It's not the speaking really, it's the reading and writing.'

Gwen paused in her chores and rested her rubber glove hands on the side.

'I wouldn't be much help. I haven't written in Welsh for years. We only moved back last year so I haven't had much practice. It's a common thing in these parts. Most people can speak the language but there's not so much cause to write in it.'

Sophie did her best to hide her disappointment. She really had thought she had found her solution. She was even going to offer to pay Gwen, although it wouldn't have been much. It wasn't as if Sophie could afford to pay for a Welsh teacher.

'There are a couple of people in these parts who do teach it, the local teachers for one. It's required in all schools — but I guess you already know that,' Gwen added, with a look of sympathy.

'Thanks, but I can't really afford to pay the rates of a qualified teacher. Do you know anyone else? Someone who might be able to help that I could work in kind for?'

Gwen turned her attention back to the washing up. Sophie could see by the look on her face that she was racking her brains.

'I can think of one person,' she said finally. Sophie's heart dropped. She knew what Gwen was going to say.

'He made a promise to help you, Sophie. You helped him more than anyone else has been able to and certainly more than that Rebecca.'

Sophie shook her head. 'No it's fine. I'm doing pretty well on my own. I'll be fine.'

Sophie wasn't sure who she was trying to convince. She knew that Gwen was studying her expression, so she forced herself to smile.

'No, Sophie. He is going to keep helping you. If I have to drag him over to your van myself.'

'He hasn't actually said he won't, Gwen. It's more how awkward it would be. I'm not sure how Rebecca would feel . . . '

Sophie didn't get to finish her sentence, as she knew she needed David to help her whether she liked it or not. She tried to focus on how much she needed the help, how this was the only way she could reach her goal — but all she could think about was the agony of spending time with the man she had thought was the one, when he was no longer a possibility.

14

Sophie had got through the day at work and managed to avoid seeing David at all. She suspected after the events of the morning that he was probably trying to avoid her, too. Gwen had told her that David would be at her van for seven o'clock to help her with her Welsh, and as a result Sophie hadn't been able to settle. She couldn't face cooking herself some tea, so instead had made toast and marmite, which seemed to form part of her staple diet these days. She had fed Maple with some of the food David had given her and promised Maple and herself that she would go food shopping the next day. Even owing David for cat food seemed unbearable.

She stopped pacing when there was a knock at the door. She took a deep breath and a moment to compose herself and then went to open the door. She had decided that she was going to be cool and calm and not allow them to discuss anything that wasn't about reading or writing Welsh. She opened the door and she could see that David wanted to be there about as much as she wanted him there.

'You could have asked,' David said as he stepped inside. 'You didn't need to go via my mum.'

'I didn't exactly ask her,' Sophie said, trying to keep her voice even. 'In fact, I asked her if she would be able to help me, but she said that she hadn't written or read anything Welsh for years.'

For a moment, Sophie thought that David had frowned but it was gone before she could decide one way or the other.

'Well, I'm happy to help. I only stopped coming round because you wouldn't open the door.'

Sophie felt herself blush.

'I'm not surprised that you wouldn't let me in,' he said hurriedly. He looked like he was going to say more, and so Sophie held up her hand. This was not the plan.

'I'd really like it if we could just focus on the Welsh. I'm pretty behind on where I ought to be by now.'

David sat down and picked up a piece of translation she had been working on.

'Of course,' he said. 'Whatever you want.'

Sophie felt like the temperature in the van had dropped to winter levels. She held in a sigh. He really had no right to be all wounded soldier about this. It was, after all, mainly his fault. How was it that some people could turn a situation around so that they were the injured party? It really wasn't fair.

The evening passed quickly after that. David was all business, and although it caused a pang in Sophie's heart at how much things had changed, on the whole she was glad of it.

'Have a look at pages forty-nine and

fifty. I can do the same time tomorrow if that works for you?'

'Rebecca won't mind?'

The words slipped out before Sophie had much of a chance to think about them.

She could feel David stare at her and she wished she could take the words back.

'It's nothing to do with Rebecca,' David said haughtily, and Sophie could see again the David from that first day. She felt like she was losing him, the real David, and in that moment she thought she would cry. She steeled herself with a thought. The real David had never been hers and therefore she had nothing to lose.

'Okay, then. Tomorrow at seven,' she forced herself to say, and turned away from him, busying herself in tidying up the coffee mugs, worried what she might see on his face if she looked at him.

★ ★ ★

Sophie finished her list of chores early the next day. Without the distraction of David's company there was not much else for it than to get her head down and work through the list. As she worked, she forced herself to focus on the future. Any thoughts of David were pushed firmly from her mind as they brought with them the all-too-familiar sense of misery. Instead, she thought about the start of the course, which was the start of the big adventure. The start of her future. It seemed to have lost some of its sparkle, but Sophie knew it was just because the last few weeks had been so rough.

Teaching was what she had always wanted to do, and no man was going to make her change her mind or steal her dream from her, not for a second time. She had spent enough of her life recovering from failed relationships and there was no way that this time — which in truth could hardly be called a failed relationship, since it had barely had the opportunity to get off the ground — was going to be allowed to have the same impact.

On her way back to her van, Sophie decided that she was going to sit down and do one of the sample exams that David had brought for her. They had been hidden away in a cupboard, since their presence seemed to cause a wave of fear in Sophie, but this afternoon she was going to give it a go. Time was getting short now, and she knew she needed to see how far she had come and, perhaps more importantly, how much further she needed to go.

Sophie got herself all set up. She had the exam paper carefully laid on the table with a pencil and sharpener. Her alarm clock was on the side and set to go off in an hour and a half. With a deep, calming breath she took her seat and picked up her pencil. Maple seemed to be aware that Sophie was doing something important, so sat curled up on the back of the sofa and studied her quietly, as if taking on the role of exam invigilator.

The alarm bell made her jump, which was ridiculous since her eyes had strayed to the clock every five minutes since she had started. She knew she hadn't answered all of the questions but, looking down at the paper, she knew it would have to do. If she was going to make this a real test then she needed to see what she could do in the time.

The mock exams came with a marking guide, and so Sophie, finding a red pen, started to mark. Avoiding the temptation to be overly generous to herself, she added up her mark. Forty eight percent, which was the equivalent of a 'D' grade. She tried to ignore the wave of panic that came with the knowledge she would need to achieve at least a 'B' grade in order to meet the requirements for her course.

'It's fine,' she said to Maple, who did not look convinced. 'If I'd tried this when I arrived, I wouldn't have been able to do any of it. I just need to compile a list of the areas I need to work on, and then go ahead and work on them.'

Maple did a slow blink and then strolled over for a stroke.

'You're right. David will help me. I'll show him the papers tonight and he can help me with where I went wrong. It will be fine,' she said, knowing that she was trying to convince herself.

Sophie worked steadily for the rest of the afternoon, tackling grammar and spelling, then went off to the supermarket. She needed cat food and didn't think she could face more toast and marmite. She also thought she would make some snacks for her and David to eat during their evening session, wondering if it would help them both relax and lighten the mood a little.

Pulling into the space beside her van, she could see Maple sat on the front door step. She pulled the bags of shopping out of the boot and couldn't help but look over to David's van, which seemed quiet and still. She shrugged to herself. Perhaps he and

Rebecca had gone out for an early dinner.

Maple greeted her arrival by winding around her legs, which made it difficult to get into the van without dropping bags of shopping, but Sophie was well practised. She also knew how to distract her cat, and put a plate of her favourite food down so that she could get on with her unpacking and put together the snacks she had brought. She wondered if David would have room if he had been out for food, but since she had also brought a couple of bottles of his beer, she figured she might be able to tempt him.

At seven she was all ready to go. The snacks were laid out, the beers were in the fridge, but there was no sign of David. This was not a major surprise, since he was not the best time-keeper she had ever met, so she sat at the table and got back to her Welsh, knowing that she didn't really have the time to sit around and wonder where he was.

At seven-thirty she was officially

distracted, looking at her watch and then at the van, which showed no signs of anyone — not David or Rebecca.

'I guess he's forgotten or been held up,' Sophie said out loud. Maple yawned and stretched, turned round a few times and then sat back down.

'We did say seven but maybe he thought we agreed eight.'

She nodded and forced herself back to work.

Eight came and went, as did nine, and Sophie knew that David wasn't coming. There was no sign of him at the van and his car hadn't returned. Sophie couldn't work out what was worse, the idea that he had forgotten or that he had remembered but had chosen not to come. Not that she could blame him. She had barely spoken to him since Rebecca had arrived, and when she had the words had been angry and pointed. She hadn't let him speak, hadn't let him even try to explain and perhaps that was why he had changed his mind.

It was no good, she wasn't going to

be able to hold the tears back and since there seemed no danger of any company, she let herself cry. She cried that she had lost David, the man she had thought was the one. She cried that they didn't even seem able to be friends. Maple came and sat in her lap offering feline comfort.

In the morning, Sophie's eyes felt gritty and tired, the result of a night of tears. She forced herself out of bed and started her morning routine. She had come to a decision in the early hours and she wanted to get on with it before she chickened out. She was going to talk to David. She was going to apologise for her part in this whole mess, and most importantly, she was going to listen to what he had to say.

She knew that she wanted David to remain a part of her life, even if that meant only being friends. The thought that she would have to try and like Rebecca was less palatable, but she knew that David's friendship would be worth that sacrifice. She headed off to the showers. She knew in her head what jobs David had been allocated for the day — she had memorised it previously so she could ensure she was anywhere he wasn't, but now she was going to use it to find time to speak to him alone.

But despite the fact that Sophie had carefully planned all her jobs so that they would coincide with where she thought David would be, there was no sign of him. She forced herself to keep to her schedule, though. Gwen and Jeff had been so good to her, there was no way she was going to let them down by not doing her job, however badly she wanted to speak to David. There were certain jobs that were done at certain times so as to inconvenience the guests as little as possible. The showers and toilets, for example, were shut for cleaning at eleven a.m. every day for half an hour, so that you had to stick to. Sophie was down to clean the ladies and David the gents, so she was bound to see him there.

As she ticked off her list of pitches

and vans that needed to be cleaned and checked, ready for the next visitors, she practised what she wanted to say. She knew she had a habit of starting with what she intended to say and then basically apologising for everything the other person had done and she was determined not to do that this time. Instead, she was going to explain to David what she had thought about Rebecca but also admit that he had never specifically said that she was dead. She wondered if they would laugh a little at her assumption and perhaps that would be the start of them rediscovering their friendship. Maybe even Rebecca would find it funny. An image of Rebecca swam into Sophie's mind, haughty and unamused. Perhaps not, she thought. That in itself made her smile and, not for the first time, wonder at David and Rebecca being together. They seemed so different, incompatible even. Maybe opposites really did attract?

A man in a towelling dressing gown

walked past, holding a wash bag. He stared at her curiously and then hurried away. Sophie realised that she had laughed out loud, seemingly at nothing, and must look slight deranged. So she straightened her face and headed in the direction of the toilets. When she arrived, there was no sign of David. She put up the sign to inform guests that the toilets were now closed for cleaning and then heard the tell tale sounds of the cleaning trolley heading towards the other half of the building that housed the gents.

Giving herself no time to chicken out she walked around the building.

'Morning, pet.'

Sophie froze. Lydia was standing there, pulling on rubber gloves and clearly preparing to clean.

'Morning, Lydia,' Sophie said, forcing a smile on to her face. 'I thought David was on the rota for this.'

Sophie tried to keep her voice casual but knew that she wasn't succeeding.

'He was supposed to be. Gwen's

right frantic. She needed to speak to him about taking Jeff up to the hospital for his fracture clinic appointment but there was no sign of him at the van and his car was gone. She tried to call him, but no answer. Looks like he's just up and left with that Rebecca girl, without so much as a word to his parents.'

15

Sophie swallowed and did her best not to look stricken by the news. Not easy, since she felt like she had just eaten a whole tray of ice cubes.

She put out a hand out and leaned on the trolley.

'I'm guessing by the look on your face that he didn't bother to tell you he was leaving either?' Lydia said, leaning over and patting her on the arm. 'And after all you've done for him. I really thought he'd changed, but that Rebecca comes back on the scene and the old David's back as soon as she clicks her fingers.'

'Well, I'd best be getting on,' Sophie managed to croak. She had an over-whelming urge to be on her own, and right now, cleaning the toilets seemed like it would provide her with that kind of sanctuary.

'Of course, sweetheart,' Lydia said, with such a look of sympathy that Sophie thought she would cry.

'If you need any help with any of . . . ' Sophie couldn't bring herself to say the name out loud. ' . . . his jobs, then let me know.'

Sophie turned away and forced herself to put one foot in front of the other.

'And if Paul and I can do anything, just shout . . . '

The rest of Lydia's words were drowned out by the swing door to the ladies closing.

Mechanically, Sophie checked every stall and cubicle to ensure that she was alone. She had checked that the 'No entry' sign was on the door. Once she was sure she was alone, she chose a toilet cubicle, shut the lid, sat down and cried.

As her sobs started to subside, Sophie checked her watch. She had been crying for exactly twelve minutes and it was time, she told herself firmly, to get a grip. She pulled off another piece of toilet roll and dried the last of her tears. Perhaps thinking they would be the very last of her tears ever was a little hopeful, but she could at least keep it together until she had finished all her jobs and was in the privacy of her own van. She walked out of the cubicle and caught sight of herself in the wall of mirrors. It was not a pretty sight so she splashed her face with cold water, took a deep breath and fetched her rubber gloves.

When Sophie had finished all her jobs, tired and in need of a shower, she trudged back to her van. Maple was sat on the steps to David's van and when she saw Sophie started to meow plaintively. Sophie walked over and tickled Maple behind her ears.

'He's gone,' Sophie said. 'Maybe forever, so we need to get over it,' she added and looked at her cat. Maple was clearly not convinced.

'I guess he closed the window on you?' Sophie asked and was rewarded with an affirmative chirp.

'Did you look inside, through the window, I mean?' Sophie asked, and exchanged a look with Maple. She jumped up, and with Maple trotting at her heels she walked around the side of the van, grabbing the steps and putting them underneath the window that was usually Maple's entrance. Together, they climbed the steps and peered through the window.

It was not good news.

Even through the window, Sophie could see that David hadn't just planned to be away for a few days. The wardrobe door was open and empty. There were no piles of shoes on the floor and all the books were gone from the bookcase. David was gone, and by the looks of it he had no plans to return. Sophie wasn't sure how long she had stood at the top of the steps and stared. She could perhaps understand that he wanted to leave, to return to his old life, but what she couldn't get her head around was the fact that he had left without a word. He hadn't even told his parents he was leaving; he had just disappeared in the middle of the night. Disappeared like a coward, not willing to face any of them with his decision to go.

Sophie clenched her fists, her nails biting into the palms of her hands. The anger was pushing away the sadness. It was more evidence, if more evidence was needed, that David had deceived her, with his feelings and with his promises to help her.

She took a deep breath, clicked her tongue at Maple in the hopes that she would follow, and headed back to her van. She realised she was even more determined now. She was going to achieve her goal and she was going to do it without David's help. A man had broken her heart before and it had cost her two years of her life, but she learnt from the experience and she wasn't going to let that happen again.

'There will be no wallowing, Maple,' she said as she stepped inside. 'For one thing, we don't have time. I have a Welsh exam in two weeks. And for another thing,' she said as she grabbed the cat treats and sprinkled a few on the floor, 'he is clearly not worth it.'

For the next two weeks, Sophie worked like she had never worked before. She studied before starting her day's jobs and afterwards late into the evening. Gwen had taken to bringing Sophie lunch and dinner, clearly convinced that if she didn't, Sophie wouldn't bother to eat.

The morning of the dreaded exam arrived, and Sophie had been awake for hours. She knew that she had done all she could, but couldn't help having a quick look at her Welsh grammar book. Maple was sat on the table staring at her intently.

'Yes I know, if I don't know it by now I never will,' she said, reaching out to scratch Maple under the chin. 'Wish me luck. We'll have some tuna tonight to celebrate.'

Maple cocked her head to one side.

'However well it goes, we'll celebrate. I promise.'

Sophie checked her watch for the thousandth time that morning and picked up her bag.

'I'll be early, but then I can go and get a coffee and hopefully calm down a bit.'

Maple reached out a paw, which Sophie took to be a sign of encouragement. She headed out to her car. As she drove slowly out of the campsite, she came to the small office. There was a large, hand-painted banner with 'Good Luck Sophie!' written on it, and in smaller writing underneath: 'not that you need it!' Sophie couldn't help but smile, and she waved at Gwen and Jeff who were standing outside waiting to see her off with an enthusiastic grin. She wound down her window and promised faithfully to come back to the office and tell them all about it when she was done.

As Sophie drove away, she made herself focus on all the good luck messages she had received in postcards and letters — her friends and family knew that the phone signal at the campsite was non-existent — and the support of Gwen and Jeff. She made a conscious effort to push any thoughts of David from her mind. When his image swung into her vision, she reached out and switched on the CD player and listened to an audiobook that was recorded in Welsh, thinking it might help tune her brain into the language.

Sophie pulled into an almost empty car park outside one of the University buildings. The term wasn't due to start for another few weeks and so it was likely that the other couple of cars belonged to potential students like herself. She picked up her bag and headed to the main door which had a sign on it directing the students sitting the Arholiad Cymraeg to make their way to Classroom 4. The classroom was empty. Sophie had passed a small seating area with a coffee vending machine, so she decided to go and wait there. One look at her watch told her there was just less than an hour before the exam was due to start.

Not unexpectedly, the coffee was dire, but Sophie drank it anyway, for something to do more than anything else. An older woman had arrived, given her a quick smile and then pulled out a notebook full of handwritten notes. She clearly did not want to make small talk. She was followed by several other students who seemed to be of the same mindset, and so Sophie sat and re-read the posters hanging on the wall advertising various clubs and societies that you could join if you were a student, and wondered if she would ever get the chance. She felt foolish for not bringing anything with her to study, but at least the posters were in Welsh so she was doing something to keep her mind on the subject at hand.

About ten minutes before the exam was due to start, the front door slammed and a man, who looked like a surfer with too-long, dirty blond hair and blue eyes made his entrance.

'Did you see all that traffic? I thought I was going to be stuck on the Menai Bridge forever.'

Most of the other students ignored him but Sophie smiled at him. She'd had a similar experience herself on previous occasions. She watched as he took in their fellow students, shrugged and then sat down on the free seat beside her.

'Joe Evans,' he said, holding out a hand and smiling.

There was a twang to his accent that Sophie couldn't place.

'Sophie Carson,' she replied, shaking his hand, which felt rough beneath hers.

'Here for the Welsh exam?' he asked with a grin. It seemed doubtful that anyone was there for anything else.

'Yep,' Sophie said with a grimace. 'You?'

'Yeah. I'm pretty rusty. I grew up here, but we moved to South Africa when I was twelve so I haven't had much practice.'

Sophie raised her eyebrows. Now the slight accent made sense.

'I'm in the same boat. I used to spend my summer holidays here with my grandparents, so speaking Welsh is fine, but writing and reading is more of a challenge.'

Joe nodded in agreement.

'It's a brutal language. I'm just hoping I can pass this thing,' he said, waving his hand in the direction of the classroom. 'My place on the course depends on it.'

'Me too,' Sophie said. 'I'm on the one year postgraduate primary teaching course.'

'Heritage Studies,' Joe said, grinning.

'You need Welsh for that too?'

Sophie was surprised. She had always thought it was just if you wanted to teach in north Wales that you needed to speak the language.

''Fraid so. Makes sense, since most people up here in the north speak the language. Also means that I get a grant towards the fees.' He said this with a twinkle in his eye. 'To be honest, I'd be pushed to afford it without the extra money.'

'Me too,' Sophie said. She couldn't quite believe that their situations were so similar.

They didn't have a chance to talk much more as a lecturer appeared with a pile of exam papers and directed them to the classroom.

'Do you fancy a coffee after?' Joe said as they walked along the corridor.

'I'd love to,' Sophie said. If coming hundreds of miles away from her family and friends had been slightly crazy, then at least she wasn't the only one.

16

The exam had two parts, first reading and then writing. The four hours seemed to fly by, and in no time, Sophie found herself back out in the small reception area waiting for Joe.

'I'm glad that's over. How do you think you did?' he asked.

'Honestly, I've no idea,' Sophie said. 'I can barely remember what the questions were.'

He grinned at her.

'Post-exam amnesia. It's the way to go, not like you can do anything about it now.' He rubbed his hands together. 'I don't know about you, but I'm starving. You up for that coffee and maybe something to eat?'

'That would be great. I'm not working today.'

'I know a place with plenty of parking and great all-day breakfasts. Follow me.'

Sophie followed Joe to a small café bar on the outskirts of Bangor. It was clearly a student hangout, with posters advertising events for the upcoming Freshers' Week, with live music and cheap drinks. Joe took a narrow side street and pulled his elderly Mini into a parking spot. Sophie parked next to him and climbed out of her car.

'Doesn't look much, but the food's great and if your budget is anything like mine then you'll be able to afford to actually eat for the rest of the week as well.'

Joe grinned. He had a wide, toothy smile that seemed to shine from his tanned face. He wasn't exactly handsome in the traditional sense, but he seemed to embrace who he was and Sophie felt drawn to him.

'So, why Wales?' Sophie said after they had ordered.

'We went to South Africa for my dad's job back in 'ninety-nine. I was all up for it, having lived on Anglesey up till then. Ready for a new adventure.

But strange as it may sound, Wales has always felt like home.'

Sophie nodded. She had never lived in Wales permanently, but she felt exactly the same.

'I mean, I loved the landscape and the wildlife is amazing, as is the surfing.'

Sophie couldn't help but giggle, and Joe's eyebrows lifted into a quizzical expression.

'Sorry, it's just that you do scream surfer.'

Joe looked away from her to a mirror on the wall as if it had only just occurred to him.

'Do you think so?' he asked, with a mischievous look in his eye.

'Oh, please. You know you do.'

Joe shrugged. 'Well, the ladies seem to like it.'

Now it was Sophie's turn to raise an eyebrow.

'The ladies?'

Joe laughed. 'You know what I mean. It's not like I can compete with the conventional male model thing.'

Sophie laughed, shaking her head. Speaking to Joe was refreshing, he was so open and honest. Unlike David, a small voice said in her head. The thought of David made her frown.

'You okay?' Joe asked, looking a little concerned.

Sophie shook herself. 'I'm fine. I was just thinking about how much you don't remind me of someone.'

'And I take it that's a good thing?'

'You have no idea,' Sophie said as their coffees arrived.

'Would that be an ex-someone?'

Sophie took a sip to give her a chance to think. This was not what you were supposed to do when you met someone new.

'Didn't really get to being an ex,' she said finally.

'Ah. And I'm guessing you don't really want to talk about it?'

Sophie could feel he was looking at her closely and he seemed to understand.

'Not really,' she answered, with a shrug.

'Are you sure, because I have some pretty horrific stories of past relationships that I'm quite sure will make your experiences pale in comparison.'

Sophie choked on her coffee and had to reach for one of the paper napkins.

'Oh, really?' she said, coughing a little.

'Oh, yes. You're choking now, but you wait. Seriously, it's like some terrible gothic horror story of failed and doomed romance. You'll laugh, you'll cry, you'll marvel at my hapless attempts at wooing the opposite sex.'

Sophie could feel herself relax. Maybe it would be good to hear about someone else's tragic love life, and Joe seemed happy to share.

'Go on then. You tell me yours and then I'll tell you mine. It'll be like a competition to see which of us has the worst love life.'

'Only if you're sure. Some of my tales should come with a rating for misery.

You know, only suitable for over eighteens and those who have a positive outlook on life.'

'I'm sure I'll cope,' Sophie said with a smile.

'Okay then,' Joe said, stretching his arms as if he were preparing for some intensive exercise. He rolled his shoulders and took a few deep breaths. Sophie just watched in amusement, before sighing, which seemed to spur him on.

'So, first there was Tina.'

He turned his gaze to look out of the window onto the narrow street in such a parody of romantic loss that Sophie had to fight the urge to kick his shin under the table.

'Tina,' she prompted, thinking that if she didn't, this heartbroken act might go on forever.

'Tina. She had such blonde hair it was almost white, and it was so fine that from a distance she looked like she had no hair at all.'

Sophie laughed and swallowed a

mouthful of coffee at the same time, and ended up coughing so hard that her eyes watered and she had to reach for a napkin. Joe didn't seem to notice, he was so caught up in his story.

'We were doomed from the start. Our families didn't get on, you see, or at least, our mothers didn't, and knowing our families didn't approve finally drove us apart. That, and the fact that neither of us could actually drive.'

Sophie thought about what Joe had said. 'Hang on, how old were you?'

'Oh, about eighteen months. Our mothers were in the same antenatal class but never really got on.'

'Your first love was eighteen months old?'

'Hmm,' Joe said, with a wistful look in his eye. 'My first older woman. She was born eleven days before me, but we never let the age gap get in our way.'

Now Sophie laughed. Joe was ridiculous but she had to admit that he was exactly what she needed in her life right now. Someone who would make her laugh and forget about everything else that had happened recently. Her sister was right, she needed to have some fun and try and move on.

'So, what happened?' Sophie said, trying to mirror his serious expression but failing miserably, as her smile would just not stay off her face.

'I believe there was an argument over whose turn it was to bring biscuits to mother and baby group. My mum never really told me what happened.' He looked at Sophie and managed a mournful expression. 'Too painful, I guess. I sometimes wonder if I am a constant reminder of the pain of being accused of such a heinous crime.'

'Forgetting to buy biscuits?' Sophie said, giggling.

'Indeed. You have no idea how seriously these things are taken in the world of mother and baby groups, or I suspect you would not be laughing now.'

Joe was the master of expression, as now he managed to look reproachful.

Sophie put a hand over her mouth to hide her smile.

'It's no good, you know. I can tell you're laughing. Your eyes give it away.' Joe grinned back at her. 'You have a great laugh. You should do it more often.

'There hasn't been a whole lot to laugh about lately, if I'm honest.'

Joe studied her and then waved a hand at the waitress, who was dressed in jeans and a T-shirt that bore the logo of the café bar.

'Could we have a pot of tea, please?' Joe said, glancing at Sophie, who nodded and wondered if Joe could read her mind. 'And perhaps some cakes?'

The waitress smiled and went off to fill the new order.

'I think we'll need to keep our strength up, especially when I get to my high school years. The tragedy really starts to kick in there. Unless you want to tell me about yours?' he asked.

Sophie shook her head. 'No, you're on a roll and should probably keep going. My love life is not nearly so dramatic and, I suspect, significantly shorter.'

Now Joe shrugged. 'What can I say? I'm lover not a fighter.'

Sophie laughed again, wondering what he could come up with next.

★   ★   ★

'So here I am. That's me.' Joe leaned back in his chair with his hands behind his head.

'Wow,' was about all Sophie could think to say. There had been plenty of humour in Joe's tales, but there were clearly some genuinely painful experiences too. Experiences that made Sophie feel hers paled into comparison. Joe tilted his head to one side and gazed at her. She met his gaze and waited, knowing he was going to say something, but he just hadn't quite figured out how to do it.

'So I was wondering if you fancied getting together again some time. I have a few friends who still live round here, but it would be good to have a friend once Uni starts.'

Sophie didn't really have to think about that. She liked Joe, and she could certainly do with a friend right now, particularly one who could make her laugh so easily.

'I'd like that.'

'Great,' Joe said. 'Apparently the results should be posted out to us next Friday. How about we save opening our letters until we get together? Then we can either celebrate or commiserate?'

'I know just the place,' Sophie said, thinking of the Pirate's Rest café on the beach. She wondered if it would be weird to meet Joe there, having only ever been with David. But it was such an amazing place and surely it would be a good sign that she was moving on if she could go back there without getting upset.

'Here's my email address,' he said, pulling out a biro and scribbling on the back of a thin paper napkin. 'Send me the details and I'll meet you there. Or I could come pick you up?'

'Probably best to meet there. If you come and collect me you'll be going miles out of your way.'

Sophie didn't say out loud that she wasn't sure she was ready for Gwen and Jeff to see her with another man, even if that man was simply a friend.

Joe nodded, and Sophie wondered if he had guessed some of her story. She felt a sudden reluctance to tell him about it and it must have shown on her face.

'Why don't we save your romantic tales of woe for next time as well?'

Sophie nodded. Despite the fact she felt as if she had known Joe for much longer than just a day, and that his stories told her he would likely be a sympathetic listener, Sophie wasn't sure she was ready to tell him about David. It all seemed so raw, particularly on the day she had sat her Welsh exams; a day that would have been a lot less stressful if he had kept his promise to help her.

She couldn't help wondering how easy it had been for him to walk away from something that he knew was so important to her, especially after he'd said how he felt about her, and what she had told him about her own feelings.

A small part of her thought there had to be a good reason for him disappearing without a word in the middle of the night, but she couldn't for the life of her think what that might be. She had thought that she knew David, that she understood him, but clearly she'd been wrong. It wasn't as if it was the first time in her life she had made that mistake. She needed to be more careful with her heart. That thought made her look at Joe. He was sat quietly, giving her the space to think. Or maybe she was just reading him wrong. If history told her anything, it was that she was not the best judge of character.

'Can we have the bill, please?' Joe said as the waitress passed by with a pile of dirty plates. 'Are you okay?' he asked, turning his attention to Sophie. 'I know it may not seem like it but I'm a pretty good listener if you want to talk. No pressure.'

Sophie studied his face, which seemed open and honest, and made up her mind.

'To be honest, I'm not really sure what the story is yet. I feel like I need to figure things out in my own head first.'

The bill arrived and Sophie insisting on paying her half. It wasn't like they were on a date, and Joe had been right — the prices were a relief in light of her cash-strapped budget. Joe, for his part, had seemed happy to pay the whole bill or just his half.

'So you'll send me the details for next week?' Joe said as they stood in the car park by their cars.

'I will. I think you'll like it.'

'It's going to be a long week waiting for those results. I'm glad I'll have someone to share it with and I have to say I'm intrigued by this best place on the island promise.'

'You won't be disappointed,' Sophie said with a smile. Although the thought of that official-looking envelope arriving at the campsite office filled her with dread, Joe was right — it would be good to share it with someone who really understood the significance. It sounded as if Joe had as much to lose or gain as she did.

'Great. I'll see you Friday then,' Joe said, and got in his car. Sophie did the same and watched him drive off, feeling as if she had a lot to think about.

17

Despite Sophie's fears, the week passed quickly. The site was fully booked, as it was the height of the school holidays, and being one person down meant there was plenty of work to keep Sophie occupied. She had avoided seeing Gwen and Jeff, which she felt badly about, but at the same time she didn't really want to hear if they'd had any news from David. Sophie had swapped her day off without incident — as soon as she had explained to Lydia that her results were arriving that day, Lydia had readily agreed to swap days.

The morning arrived. Sophie had been awake most of the night. At around four a.m. she had given up, switched on the bedside light and tried to read. Her mind wandered constantly and she was glad when the sun finally made an appearance. After a quick shower, and with no appetite for breakfast, she had relocated to the camp office where the post was delivered.

'Morning, Sophie. No need to ask why you're here so early. Today's the day is it?' Jeff said from his perch on the stool behind the office desk. He was out of plaster now but wore a surgical boot and still needed crutches.

Sophie couldn't make her mouth form words that would answer and so she just nodded. Gwen bustled in from the back room.

'Is that Sophie?'

Sophie managed a smile.

'Ah, there you are pet. Have you had breakfast?' Gwen asked, in a motherly way.

'No, but I don't think I could eat a thing.'

'Nonsense. You can't be celebrating good news on an empty stomach, now can you?' And with that, Gwen disappeared out the back and Sophie could hear noises that suggested breakfast was being prepared, whether she liked it or not.

'No point arguing, lass. When Gwen can't do anything about the situation, she resorts to feeding people.'

'She's very kind. It's just that I'm so nervous. This is really important.'

Jeff reached out and took Sophie's hand and gave it a squeeze.

'We know it is, love, but you've worked really hard. I'm sure you will do just fine.'

They sat together in companionable silence as Gwen cooked and Jeff checked the site computer for booking emails. The bell over the door rang and the postman appeared. He held out a handful of different-sized envelopes wrapped in an elastic band and Sophie took them with a shaky hand. She swallowed the hard lump that had formed in her throat and manged to squeeze out a quiet 'Thank you.'

'Is that the post?' Gwen called from the back.

'Yes, love,' Jeff said as he watched Sophie sort through the pile.

For a moment she thought the letter wasn't there. She had never considered that the post might be delayed, or that perhaps there had been a problem at the University which had prevented them sending it out. But then she reached the last envelope, which had the embossed crest of the University beside the postmark.

'Are you going to open it, Sophie, or just stare at it?' Gwen said from the doorway, and to be fair, she looked as nervous as Sophie felt.

'Leave her be, Gwen,' Jeff said.

'Actually, I've arranged to meet a friend later and we're going to open them together,' Sophie said, suddenly feeling a bit bad that she was going to make them wait as well. She watched as Jeff gave Gwen a look and whatever Gwen was about to say died on her lips.

'Good for you. You celebrate with your friends and when you're done, come back here and we'll celebrate some more,' said Jeff, and he smiled at Sophie and then turned his attention back to the computer.

'Thank you, really, both of you. You've been so good to me. I promise I will be back later and tell you all about it.'

And with that, Sophie headed back to her van.

'Who's this friend, that's what I want to know,' Gwen said.

'It's good that she's made a new friend. I've been worried about her since David upped and left,' Jeff said. 'But I think the boy has finally seen sense . . . There's an email here from him. Maybe he's going to explain what on earth he's been up to.'

Gwen marched over.

'Why didn't you say so before?' she said. 'Sophie might want to know what's going on.'

Jeff shook his head. 'I wanted to know what his excuses were before I shared them with Sophie. She's been upset enough as it is, and if he is back with Rebecca I don't think we want to be ruining this day for her. Do you?'

Gwen looked put out, but stepped over and gestured for Jeff to open the email. She leant over his shoulder and together they read the message from their son.

* * *

The letter felt heavy in her hand and, like ripping off a plaster, she had a sudden urge to tear it open and to know what it contained. She was stuck in that strange place of both wanting to know and also wanting to put off knowing as long as possible. An image of Joe swam into her mind, and she knew that she wasn't going to open her letter. They had agreed to open them together and that's what she was going to do. She just needed to fill up a couple of hours of her time, which she had already decided that she would do by cleaning the van from top to bottom.

By the time she had finished, she

needed another shower. To keep her mind from obsessing over her results, she had worked with the kind of zeal usually reserved for when she knew she had visitors coming. Glancing at her watch, she knew that she had reached the time she could reasonably leave without being hopelessly early. She grabbed her car keys and the letter, which she had propped up against the teapot, said good bye to Maple, and headed for her car.

Sophie had printed off a map, just in case, but found the small hill-top car park without any difficulties. She scanned the few cars that were also parked and spotted Joe's. Stepping out of her car, she walked over and banged on the window. He was sat in the driver's seat, with his envelope resting on the steering wheel and his eyes fixed upon it, as though if he concentrated hard enough, he would be able to read the contents inside without actually opening it.

Sophie banged on the window and

Joe jumped. Unsure whether he was messing with her or not, she rolled her eyes. He opened the car door and waved the envelope at her.

'Did you get yours?'

'Yes, it's in here.' She patted her small leather shoulder bag.

'Let's do it then, I don't think I can wait any longer.' Joe was actually bouncing up and down on the spot.

'I'm sure you can wait till we get to the café. It's pretty blowy up here and knowing my luck the wind will take my letter before I've had a chance to read it.'

As if on cue, a gust of wind roared up the cliff, making their hair dance, and Joe nearly lost a grip on his precious envelope. He quickly tucked it away inside his jacket and laughed sheepishly.

'Looks like you're right. Can I expect that to be a common trend?'

Sophie laughed. 'Let's just say I've had plenty of experience of the whole what-can-go-wrong-will-go-wrong thing.'

They walked along the cliff and

Sophie kept an eye out for the set of steps that would take them down to the beach.

'Since I'm almost dying of anticipation here, perhaps you could regale me with your tragic romantic story. You've heard mine and I think you'll agree it can't be that bad.'

'It's certainly a lot shorter,' she said with a snort. Then, with a sigh, she started the story at the beginning with Steve, her first love.

Joe was true to his word, he was a good listener. For starters, he didn't interrupt or offer advice, he just let Sophie talk. In no time, they had made their way along the beach and were standing outside Pirate's Rest.

'I can't believe I lived here all those years and never knew this was here!'

Sophie laughed. 'That was my reaction. You wait till you get inside.'

They found a table near to the window, so that they could take in the incredible views of the beach. Remembering how popular and busy it was

217

there, Sophie had purposely suggested they meet for an early lunch.

'So, that was Steve — but I'm guessing that's not the end of the story?'

Sophie nodded as she studied the menu, even though she knew exactly what she was going to order — the same as last time, since it had been so delicious.

'The not-quite-an-ex?' Joe prompted.

'I thought you were desperate to find out your results. Let's open our letters and we can come back to my disappointing love life later.'

'Oh no,' Joe said. 'You can't leave me hanging like that. I want to know what happened next. Seriously, it's gripping stuff. You should write a novel.'

Sophie giggled, despite the dread she felt at trying to explain what had happened between her and David.

'You're the creative one! All those girls and women you claim to have loved. If you ask me, you know a lot more about romance than I do.'

'Doomed romance, perhaps, but since I have a string of failed relationships I could hardly be called an expert. Unless, of course, you want advice on how not to do it.'

The waitress arrived with their coffees and took their food order.

'Go on, then. I'm not opening my letter till you tell me the whole sorry tale.'

Sophie sighed. Joe was like a dog with a bone.

'Fine, but it's all a bit ridiculous, really.'

Joe raised an eyebrow and said nothing. Sophie knew that unless she told him what had happened, she wouldn't get to open her envelope anytime soon.

'So, I came to the campsite to work through the summer and earn some money. It also meant I'd have a place I could afford to live whilst I did my course.'

'This, I know,' Joe said. 'Get onto the juicy bits!'

Sophie sipped her coffee and made a face at him.

'David, who is the son of the owners, was also working there.'

She reached out for the teaspoon and stirred her coffee, needing to do something with her hands.

'Our first meeting didn't go well. He lost my cat . . . '

'I'm sorry to interrupt, but how does someone else lose your cat?' Joe said, clearly paying close attention to the details of the story.

Sophie waved her hands impatiently. She knew she needed to just get it out, or she might chicken out.

'Maple was sat in the front seat of the car and David opened the door and scared her.'

Joe nodded, seemingly placated.

'Anyway, he yelled at me for parking where I shouldn't. I yelled at him for scaring my cat and we both threatened to call the police. It wasn't pretty.'

Joe lifted a hand to his mouth and was so clearly trying not to laugh that

Sophie kicked him under the table.

'Sorry. Carry on.'

'Anyway, he turned out to be the grumpiest, most miserable man I had ever met. He was rude and churlish and I had to work with him.'

Joe raised an eyebrow.

'Doesn't sound like a recipe for success.'

'I figured that there had to be more to it,' Sophie said, ignoring Joe's comment. 'As it turned out, I was right, sort of. David had been in relationship with a woman called Rebecca.' Sophie sighed. 'Short version is that I thought Rebecca had died, but in fact, she'd just dumped him.'

Their food arrived, and so Sophie picked up her fork and started to tuck in.

'So I decided, as I always do, because I'm an idiot . . . ' Joe made a noise which suggested he disagreed with her. ' . . . to try and help him. I thought that he was struggling to get over the death of his girlfriend and I figured he needed

221

a friend. So we started spending time together. He helped me with my Welsh and I cooked him dinner.'

Sophie put down her fork. Somehow, whenever she talked or thought about David, it seemed to kill her appetite.

'But you became more than a friend?' Joe asked.

'Sort of. He said that he liked me and thought maybe he felt more than that, but he also knew he needed time to get over Rebecca.'

'And you were okay with that? The time thing?'

'Actually, I was relieved. I thought he might be the one.' She struggled to say the words out loud, as they sounded so ridiculous now, so foolish and child-like. 'And I thought if our relationship was going to stand a chance, David needed to be with me for me, not because of a need to be with anyone just to ease the pain of Rebecca. So we agreed to be friends and not to see anyone else until we both felt we were ready to try out a relationship.'

'But Rebecca, not being dead, sort of threw a spanner in the works?'

Sophie shrugged. 'I think her turning up out of the blue and me finding out she was, in fact, alive, didn't really help things.'

'Ouch,' Joe said sympathetically.

'He never exactly said she was dead. He just talked like she was, and I just kind of assumed. It didn't seem right to just ask him outright.'

Sophie took a deep breath and clenched her fists. She was not going to cry about this, not anymore, and certainly not in front of Joe. Joe put down his knife and fork and reached across the table and lay his hand over hers.

'You don't have to tell me any more. I didn't mean to upset you.'

'You didn't,' Sophie said, managing a watery smile. 'And there's not much more to tell. Rebecca moved in with David. He promised to keep helping me with my Welsh, but the next day they were both gone. No note, no nothing.'

'Blimey, that's low. I think that even trumps my Carina story.'

Sophie laughed softly and shook her head.

'You were going out with Carina and she went off with your best friend. My relationship with David was pretty much all in my head. And he was right; he clearly wasn't over Rebecca.'

Joe's hand was still resting on hers and he gave it a squeeze.

'Different situations, but it looks to me like it was just as painful.'

The door to the café opened and, despite the sun in the sky, a cool wind blew through the open door. Sophie looked up and saw the last person on this earth that she was expecting to see.

18

Sophie pulled her hand out from under Joe's. She wasn't sure why. It wasn't as if she was doing anything wrong. It wasn't as if what she did or who she did it with was anything to do with David, but somehow the look on his face made her feel deeply guilty. David, for his part, just stood in the open doorway and stared.

Sophie found her voice first.

'David?'

She didn't really know what else to say.

Joe looked first at her, and then at the man standing in the doorway, and a look of understanding dawned on his face.

'David, lad, either out or in. The sun may be shining out there, but the wind is harsh as always,' Hywel shouted cheerfully from the kitchen area.

For a moment, Sophie was sure that he would turn around and leave. But then he took a step forward and closed the door behind him.

'I'm sorry. I'm clearly interrupting something,' David said, and his face was blank, not giving away any hint of what he was feeling.

'This is Joe,' Sophie said, feeling like she had to say something. 'We met at the exam last week.'

As soon as she said it, Sophie realised it might sound like she was being pointed, although she hadn't meant to.

'Yeah,' David said, pulling hand through his hair, and Sophie wondered if he had forgotten all about it.

Joe stood up and held out a hand to David, who seemed almost dazed. But he took it, and they shook, before Joe gestured for David to take a seat. David and Sophie stared at each other. Sophie had no idea what to say or where to start. She was dimly aware that Joe was ordering David a coffee.

'Did you get your results?' David

asked, suddenly.

Sophie blinked. He hadn't forgotten, but she wasn't sure that it meant anything. She couldn't find her voice, so simply nodded.

'We have our envelopes here,' Joe said, waving his. 'We thought we would open them together and then either celebrate or commiserate.'

'You want to be a teacher too?' David said, turning to stare at Joe.

'No. I'm into all things heritage, but I need Welsh for my degree and I also get a bursary if I pass the exam.'

David nodded, but Sophie suspected he hadn't heard a word. Joe seemed to be coping well with the awkwardness of the situation; certainly better than she was.

'So how did you do?' David asked. He directed his question to Joe, although Sophie knew he was just attempting to be polite.

'We don't know yet, we haven't opened them. We got to talking about . . .'

Sophie's voice trailed off. There was

no way she was going to tell David that she had been so distracted talking about their almost-relationship that she had yet to find out whether she'd passed the exam, whether her future was going to be delayed for another year. David sought out her gaze and Sophie found that she couldn't look away.

'Well, maybe we should open them now. Then I probably should be going,' Joe said, and Sophie felt a pang of guilt for putting her new friend in such a difficult position. Of course, it wasn't actually her fault. She'd had no idea that David would just turn up out of the blue, here of all places, when they'd all been without so much as a word from him for nearly three weeks.

'You don't have to leave,' she said firmly, and she looked at David. Either he hadn't picked up on the hint, or he didn't care. 'But you're right; let's get it over with.' Sophie pulled her envelope out of her bag and waited until Joe had picked up his.

'On the count of three?' he asked.

Sophie nodded and all that could be heard around the table was the sound of tearing paper.

'Well?' Joe asked, looking directly at her, and despite the ridiculously awkward situation that she found herself in, she couldn't help but smile.

'Seventy-two percent! I got an A!' she said out loud, not quite believing what was written in the letter, despite the number of times her eyes had scanned the key information.

'That's great, Sophie. Well done,' Joe said.

The tone of his voice made her look up from her study of the letter, and she felt intense guilt wash through her. He looked as if he was making a supreme effort to be pleased for her whilst he battled with his own results. Sophie felt her stomach drop. He hadn't got what he needed. She had spent months imagining how that would feel. Instinctively, she reached out for his hand and forced herself to ignore David. She didn't want to see his reaction, and besides, this was not about him.

'Is it that bad?' she asked.

Joe's eyes glinted.

'Well, I didn't get an A . . . but I got a B.' He shook his head now. 'I can't actually believe this. I was so sure that I flunked.'

He was grinning now, and Sophie pulled her hand away in mock anger.

'You are such a drama queen!' she said accusingly. 'From the look on your face, I was sure you had failed!'

'It was too good an opportunity to miss,' Joe said, laughing a little. 'You should have seen the look on your face!'

'Congratulations,' David said in a monotone. 'To both of you.'

Sophie turned to stare at him. How was he managing to make this about him? How dare he play the wounded person card!

'And I think that's my cue to go,' Joe said, standing up and reaching in his pocket for his wallet.

Sophie stood too.

'No, sit down Joe. We planned to celebrate together, and we're going to.'

Joe paused and looked at Sophie with an eyebrow raised, asking an unspoken question.

'Is that your not so subtle way of asking me to leave?' David said, and now he sounded like the angry man she had meet on that first day.

'No,' said Sophie though gritted teeth. 'That is my way of asking Joe not to leave, just because you have shown up unannounced.'

'I sent you an email,' David said, as if that explained everything.

'When?' Sophie said.

'Really early this morning. I said that I was going to leave straight away and see if I could get to the campsite in time for the post. So I could see you get your results.'

Sophie took a moment to digest this.

'Why?' was about the only question she could come up with. 'Why do you even care? I haven't had a word from you in weeks. You just upped and left without so much as a note. You left your parents in the lurch. You . . . ' She couldn't finish the sentence but she didn't really need to.

'If you'll just let me explain,' David said, and now he looked almost apologetic — but not enough for Sophie. All the suppressed anger and hurt boiled to the surface.

'No,' Sophie said, and stuck out her chin. 'Right now, Joe and I are going to celebrate our results. I'll be back at the site later on today, and if you're still around and you want to talk, then maybe we'll see. But right now, I think actually maybe you should leave.'

Sophie blinked, not quite believing that those words had just come out of her mouth. She had actually said what she wanted in a confrontational situation, possibly for the first time in her life. David looked taken aback and Sophie watched as his gaze switched to Joe.

'Fine,' he said abruptly, and he stood up. 'I'm clearly interrupting you and your boyfriend.'

Sophie glared at him, knowing that if she gave into the urge to speak now, she would say many things, most of which she would probably regret later. She held her breath as she watched David stomp out of the café. It wasn't lost on her that he didn't offer to pay for his untouched coffee. She let out her breath in a long, slow sigh. The truth was she didn't want to talk to David right now. She had no idea what she wanted to say, and she didn't know that she wanted to hear what he had to say. What she wanted right now was to celebrate. She had passed her Welsh exam. She was going to start on the next step to the career she had always wanted, and David wasn't going to ruin that moment.

'Well, that was awkward.'

Joe's voice cut through her thoughts, and she winced.

'I'm so sorry. I had no idea he was even in Wales, let alone that he would track me down to here.'

'He definitely wants to talk to you,' Joe said, and Sophie snorted.

'He only ever wants to talk when it suits him.' Sophie picked up the drinks menu. 'And right now, it doesn't suit me. I don't want to hear his excuses and I don't want to think about what might have been. Right now, I want to raise a glass to our achievements. How would you feel about a glass of fizz?'

'I wouldn't say no,' Joe said, looking at her closely, 'as long as you're sure? We can do this another time, or not at all if it's going to make life difficult for you and David.'

'There is no me and David. However much he might think there is. And right now, I could do with a drink.'

Sophie turned away and caught the waitress's attention. Throwing caution and budget to the wind, she ordered a glass of champagne for each of them.

Sophie felt a little light-headed with the champagne, despite the fact she had only had one small glass. She thought it was probably a combination of the lack of sleep and the nervous anticipation of her results. That, or the fact that David had suddenly reappeared on the scene. So when Joe suggested that they stroll further down the beach, she agreed.

'When does your course actually start?' Sophie asked, determined to keep the conversation away from her and David.

'Couple of weeks. There's the whole Freshers' Week thing, but I think I'm probably a bit old for all that.' He grinned at her.

'Me too. Perhaps we could compare timetables and arrange to meet up for lunch or something in our first week?'

'Sounds good to me,' Joe said in a way that made Sophie feel like there was more, but that he wasn't sure he should actually come out and say it. She stopped walking and Joe walked on ahead a little way before he noticed.

'Out with it,' she said, even as he pulled his face into an innocent frown. 'I can tell you have something to say. Spill the beans,' Sophie said, marvelling at the fact that she felt she had known Joe for years.

'I know you don't want to talk about it . . .'

Sophie cut him off.

'You're right I don't.' And she walked up to him and kept going, not waiting for him, so he had to jog to catch up.

'So why did you ask, if you knew what I was going to say?'

Sophie blew out her breath in frustration.

'I don't exactly know what you're going to say, but I'm guessing it's going to be about David. I'm just not ready to talk about that right now.'

Joe nodded as if he understood.

'But when you get back to the site, I suspect he will want to talk, and it might be good to have an idea of what you want to say.'

'Why do you care?' Sophie said sharply. 'Sorry,' she added quickly. 'I didn't mean it quite like that. More, why is it important to you?'

They walked in silence for nearly a

minute and then Joe stopped.

'I didn't tell you everything about Carina.'

'Okay,' Sophie said, with no idea where this was going.

'I had an opportunity to talk to her. She wanted to talk to me but I was hurt and angry and didn't give her the chance. I didn't give *us* a chance. Maybe things would have been different, that's all.'

He looked at her so earnestly that she knew he was not messing around.

'You're going to be wasted on the Heritage Industry. You should be an Agony Uncle.'

The seriousness was gone and his smile had returned.

'That or write some self-help books. You've got all the spiel.'

Joe nudged her in the ribs and she smiled back at him.

'So talk,' he said. 'In no particular order. How do you feel and what do you want to say?'

19

Sophie drove up to the campsite and, for the first time ever, felt like she would rather be anywhere else in the world. She and Joe had walked and talked for hours and she still wasn't sure what she wanted to say, or what she wanted to hear. For her, not enough time had passed to process her feelings. But she also knew that what Joe had said was true. She probably didn't have time to work it out by herself. Sophie was sure, now she thought about it, that if she refused to talk to David now, she would never see him again. However much she dreaded the conversation, she had decided that she wasn't one hundred percent certain that she was ready to walk away. Of course, this all assumed that David would actually be at the campsite. He was not known for controlling his temper and had obviously decided that Sophie had moved on and that Joe was her boyfriend. It would not surprise her to learn that he had left again without saying a word.

She drove slowly around the link road in the campsite, past all the families and couples sitting outside their tents and caravans, enjoying the sun but dressed up for the wind. As she completed the loop that took her back to her own van, her home, she could see that David's car was parked outside his. She pulled into her space and was instantly reminded of the first day they had met, when Maple had shot from the car and disappeared, whilst they had swapped threats to call the police. She allowed herself a minute, once parked, to decide what to do. She really ought to feed Maple, but glancing up and seeing the back window of David's van cracked open, she was pretty certain that Maple had already been fed, probably leftover sausages from breakfast.

Gripping her keys in her hand she knocked on the door.

'It's open,' came from inside the van and Sophie stepped inside, once again marvelling at how much mess David could make in such a short space of time.

David was sprawled across the long sofa at the back of the van and Maple was curled up under this chin.

Sophie waited for him to speak, but he just looked at her and she couldn't make out what he was thinking.

'You wanted to talk,' Sophie said finally, when she realised that he wasn't going to start the conversation. She felt a flash of anger at his petulance. Surely it was his place to explain what had happened, why he had made the decisions he had?

'Not sure there's much point,' he said, refusing to look at her.

Sophie rolled her eyes.

'What is that supposed to mean?' She had to fight to keep her voice even. It was only thinking about Joe's advice that made her do so.

'I wanted to talk about us, but you seemed to have moved on.'

Sophie gritted her teeth and forced the anger back down.

'You left, David. With Rebecca. I assume because you wanted to be with her.' She saw no reason to defend her own actions. She and Joe were both friends but a small part of her thought it would do David no harm to think otherwise. Then he might know how she had felt. She clenched her fists. That was childish and she knew it.

'I left, but not for the reason that you think.'

'Okay, but what was I supposed to think?'

'You were supposed to trust me.'

Sophie took a step forward, thinking that she should sit down since this conversation was going to be a long one but David didn't move his feet so she had to perch on the edge of the kitchen unit.

'I had thought Rebecca was dead . . . '

'I never said that.' He cut across her words, and sounded indignant.

'No, you didn't but you never corrected me. Are you honestly telling me that you never even suspected that I had got it wrong?'

He at least had the grace to blush.

'I wasn't sure,' he admitted. 'But I figured that Mum or Dad would have told you.'

'We're not at school, David. You can't expect your parents to step in to fix something that you should do yourself.'

The words came out crossly and Sophie watched as he flinched.

'I thought we had an agreement,' he said, moving the conversation onto ground he clearly felt was safer.

'We did!' Sophie said, raising her voice to the extent that Maple jumped off David's chest and perched near the window, ready to make a quick exit.

'You said you needed time to get over Rebecca, and I agreed. I didn't expect her to turn up and then for you to leave without a word. What did you think I would think?

She slid off the counter; she couldn't sit still.

'I thought you trusted me, but you never let me explain what was going on. I tried . . . '

Now it was Sophie's turn to cut across him. 'You tried whilst your ex-girlfriend, or current girlfriend, whatever she is, lived in your van *for two weeks*, and then you just disappeared. And you turn up today, out of the blue, and expect me to just drop everything.'

'I thought you might wait, give me a chance to explain, but then I find that you've met someone else!'

David was standing now too, and his voice was pitched at angry and getting angrier. Maple took this as her cue and disappeared out of the window with a swish of her tail.

'I can't have meant that much to you if you moved on so quickly!'

Sophie felt as if she had been slapped. She glared at him, thought about telling him that there was nothing going on between her and Joe, that they were just friends, but she was too upset, too angry. All she wanted to do was get out of the van and away from him. And so that is what she did, slamming the door behind her.

★　★　★

Sophie's alarm clock woke her and she rolled over and reached out for the snooze button. Something was wrong, but her sleep-addled brain couldn't work out what. She turned over and then realised that the familiar weight of Maple was missing. Sophie sat up and frowned. Maple hadn't been around when she had gone to bed the night before, which in itself was not unusual. But for her not to be there in the morning was definitely out of character. Sophie pulled on her clothes from the day before and checked every place in the van she could imagine her hiding. She looked out of the window to

David's van and wondered if Maple had defected to the other side. She stepped outside the van and called Maple's name softly, but there was no returning mew.

The curtains of David's van opened and Sophie could see his bleary face looking out of the window.

'You alright?' he asked groggily, and for a heartbeat it was if none of the recent events had happened.

'Sorry. Didn't mean to wake you. I don't suppose Maple is in there with you?'

He looked at her and for a moment she could see the old David, her David. But as she watched, he seemed to remember and his face crumbled into a frown before being replaced with the blank he reserved for those he was displeased with.

'Not in my room, but I'll check the van.'

Sophie waited and listened as David moved around the van. Her heart constricted as she heard his door open.

'I'll help you look,' he said, emerging in his pyjamas with a sweatshirt over the top.

They looked everywhere, calling her name, but there was no sign of Maple and Sophie was starting to panic.

'Where is she?' she said to no one in particular.

'We'll find her,' David said, with a confidence that Sophie couldn't share. She couldn't shake the feeling that something was terribly wrong.

'Let's head back to the van. She's probably there waiting for her breakfast.'

They crossed the site in silence. There was little activity at this time of the morning and Sophie couldn't think of anything beyond finding Maple.

Maple was not sat on her steps, or David's.

'Maybe we should start asking around . . . '

'Shh,' David said sharply.

Sophie couldn't help but look hurt.

'I think I hear something,' David

said, not looking at her but peering under her van.

Sophie dropped to her knees and what she saw made her feel like the world was tilting on its axis. Under her van was a bundle of fur, fur that appeared matted with a dark liquid. It was so still that Sophie was sure that Maple was gone. She stifled a sob and could feel herself start to shake. Unable to move herself, she watched as David dropped to his belly and crawled under the van.

'It's okay Maple, it's me. You're okay.'

Sophie was sure he was saying it to lessen the blow, and in that moment she felt some of the love she had forced herself to lock away escape.

'Soph. Get a towel. Maple's hurt and we need to get her to the vet.'

Sophie dashed inside and grabbed the nearest towel, and had the fore-thought to also grab her purse. Outside again, David gently lay Maple in her open arms and she wrapped her up in the towel, frightened at how cold and still Maple seemed. As she shifted herself to sit in the front seat of David's car, Maple made a low growling noise.

'It's okay Maple. It's okay. We're going to the vet and he will fix you up, you'll see.'

Sophie couldn't hold back the tears and so she sat in the car, with no idea where the nearest vet was, and sobbed into the fur of her beloved pet. Sophie was dimly aware of David's hand reaching out for her arm every time he didn't need it for driving. She wanted to thank him for taking them, despite all that had happened between them, but she couldn't find any words to say.

David opened the door to the vet's and Sophie walked through. An efficient veterinary nurse in a light blue uniform directed them into the small examination room and Sophie gently laid Maple on the table. All she could do then was whisper to Maple and try to take in what the vet was telling her.

Without knowing how she got there, she found herself sat in the waiting room with David's arm around her.

'What's happening?' she asked, straightening herself up. 'The vet was talking but I didn't really take it all in.'

David's worried face made her stomach drop once again.

'Tell me,' she asked, softly.

'It looks like Maple was hit by a car, Soph. She's in shock and has a fractured leg and pelvis. They're operating now.'

Sophie nodded, trying to take in the words.

'Maple is a fighter,' David said.

Sophie tried to nod but dissolved into yet more tears and found herself pulled into a tight hug. She stayed there, listening to David's heartbeat.

'Do you want to go and get a coffee or something? They said it will be hours.'

Sophie shook her head fiercely. She wanted to be here, she needed to be.

'What can I do?' David asked, and he sounded desperate.

'Talk to me,' Sophie said. 'Distract

me with something.'

'Okay, what do you want to talk about?' His eyes showed wariness.

Sophie sighed.

'Tell me what happened. With you and Rebecca,' she said at last. In some ways, it was the last thing she wanted to hear; but in another, it felt like the only thing that might take her mind away from Maple's fate, which she could do nothing about.

'Are you sure? I don't know if now is a good time.'

He looked at her and read her expression. After a moment's pause he started to talk.

'When Rebecca first dumped me, I was devastated. I couldn't bear to be in London without her, so I came home. I'm sorry I didn't tell you this at the time. I'm sorry I let you believe that she had died.'

''Sokay,' Sophie whispered into his chest, and she meant it. It seemed so unimportant now.

'I think everyone else was sick of me

going on about it but then you came and seemed to genuinely want to help. Selfishly, I figured if you knew the banal truth, you wouldn't be so sympathetic.'

She looked up at him now.

'My mistake,' he said, with a small, sad smile. 'I never thought she would turn up. And when she did, I didn't want her here. I didn't, I promise.'

'Then why did you invite her to stay in your van?' Sophie asked, but there was no judgement in her voice. She realised that she just wanted to know.

'I didn't,' he said ruefully. 'With Rebecca, she pretty much gets what she wants.'

'Which was you,' Sophie said. It was statement rather than a question.

'So she said.'

'And was it what you wanted?'

Sophie felt almost numbed from the overwhelming pain she was in at that moment, and didn't think more would even register.

'Honestly, I didn't know. I wanted to talk to you about it, but that night when you finally let me in, you seemed so hurt and detached.'

'So you left.'

'Not exactly. Rebecca had a phone call in the night. Her father had collapsed. They thought he might not make it through the night, so we chucked a few things in a bag and headed back to London.'

Sophie took a few moments to take this in. It made sense, sort of.

'But why didn't you just tell me that? Or tell your mum and dad?'

'Rebecca asked me not to. Her father is running as an MP in the next elections. If word got out about his health, he would never be able to run.'

Sophie pulled away from David so she could look at him. She knew her face showed incredulity. That really was a terrible excuse. David held up his hands.

'There was some truth in it, but I don't think that was her motivation,' he said at last.

'She wanted you back,' Sophie said,

shifting a little in her seat to put some distance between her and David.

His face creased in pain, but he made no move to touch her.

'Sophie, you need to understand. She wanted the old me back, the old David. When I got to London, I knew. I wasn't that person anymore. I've changed. I don't want London and my old job, my old life. And I don't want Rebecca.'

Sophie could feel fresh tears building and she knew they were not all about her.

'And what do you want?' she asked, so softly that she thought she might have to say it again.

'I want you, Soph. I want you.'

And with that, he pulled her into his arms.

Epilogue

'And how are we?' David asked, as he pulled the door to.

Sophie was sat on the sofa in their new home. David had found an old, run-down cottage in the heart of one of Sophie's favourite villages, just down the road from the campsite, and together they were doing it up.

'We're good,' Sophie said as she stroked Maple's head.

'Hello there, my favourite three-legged puss,' David said, gently picking Maple up so he could sit down next to Sophie.

Maple lifted up her head and bumped him under his chin and, as demanded, David started to smooth down her fur.

'As much the diva as ever, I see,' he said, lifting one arm to pull Sophie into a hug.

As if Maple could understand every word, she lifted a paw and patted him on the nose.

'Oh, you want to play do you?' he said, reaching down the side of the sofa and pulling out the cat toy he had made for her all those months ago, from an old sock and piece of string.

He whisked it across the floor and they both laughed as she leapt high in the air; Maple was not a cat to let losing a leg in an accident slow her down.

After ten minutes of playing, it was clear that Maple had had enough. She stretched, yawned and then meowed — a sure sign that she wanted help to get up onto the sofa. David leant forward and scooped her up.

'You know, she can do that all by herself,' Sophie said, once David had settled into the sofa again and pulled her back into his arms.

'I know,' he said softly into her hair. 'But she likes to be pampered.'

Sophie turned her face towards him

and raised an eyebrow, but couldn't hide her smile.

'Sometimes I think you love my cat more than me.'

'Not possible Sophie Carson,' David said, before leaning in and kissing her.

We do hope that you have enjoyed reading this large print book.

Did you know that all of our titles are available for purchase?

We publish a wide range of high quality large print books including:
Romances, Mysteries, Classics
General Fiction
Non Fiction and Westerns

Special interest titles available in large print are:
The Little Oxford Dictionary
Music Book, Song Book
Hymn Book, Service Book

Also available from us courtesy of Oxford University Press:
Young Readers' Dictionary
(large print edition)
Young Readers' Thesaurus
(large print edition)

For further information or a free brochure, please contact us at:
Ulverscroft Large Print Books Ltd.,
The Green, Bradgate Road, Anstey,
Leicester, LE7 7FU, England.
Tel: (00 44) **0116 236 4325**
Fax: (00 44) **0116 234 0205**

Other titles in the
Linford Romance Library:

THE SCOTTISH DIAMOND

Helena Fairfax

When actress Lizzie Smith begins rehearsals for *Macbeth*, she's convinced the witches' spells are the cause of a run of terrible luck. Her bodyguard boyfriend, Léon, is offered the job of guarding the Scottish Diamond, a fabulous jewel from the country of Montverrier. But the diamond has a history of intrigue and bloody murder; and when Lizzie discovers she's being followed through the streets of Edinburgh, it seems her worst premonitions are about to come true . . .